Dare to Touch

THE DARE TO LOVE SERIES, BOOK #3

NEW YORK TIMES BESTSELLING AUTHOR

CARLY PHILLIPS

SPENCER
HILL
PRESS

Dare to Touch
Copyright © 2015 by Karen Drogin

Please visit www.carlyphillips.com

First Edition: 2015
Carly Phillips

Dare to Touch: a novel / by Carly Phillips—1st ed.
Library of Congress Cataloging-in-Publication Data available upon request

Summary: Olivia Dare, executive director of the Miami Thunder, and team travel director, Dylan Rhodes, share more than just a passion for football—their chemistry is explosive, and their feelings for each other are intense. But Olivia is wary of any man getting too close. Given her background—a near-bigamist dad and an ex-boyfriend who merely enforced her lack of priority in his life—Olivia fears being hurt again, but she can't resist embarking upon a passionate affair with Dylan, even as she holds part of herself back.

Dylan isn't a man who does anything halfway. Once he decides to pursue Olivia, he goes all in. When the Pro Bowl takes them to the desert oasis of Arizona, Dylan is determined to make sure their time together isn't all business. What happens while at the luxury resort is life altering, but when Olivia admits her deepest pain, will Dylan be able to prove he's a man with staying power? Or will Olivia be disappointed again, this time by the most important man in her life?

Published in the United States by Spencer Hill Press
This is a Spencer Hill Contemporary Romance.
Spencer Hill Contemporary is an imprint of Spencer Hill Press.
For more information on our titles visit www.spencerhillpress.com

Distributed by Midpoint Trade Books
www.midpointtrade.com

Cover design by: Sara Eirew
Interior layout by: Scribe Inc.

ISBN: 978-1-63392-085-9
Printed in the United States of America

The Dare to Love Series and NY Dares Series

Dare to Love Series

Book 1: *Dare to Love* (Ian & Riley)
Book 2: *Dare to Desire* (Alex & Madison)
Book 3: *Dare to Touch* (Olivia & Dylan)
Book 4: *Dare to Hold* (Scott & Meg)
Book 5: *Dare to Rock* (Avery & Grey)
Book 6: *Dare to Take* (Tyler & Ella)

NY Dares Series

Book 1: *Dare to Surrender* (Gabe & Isabelle)
Book 2: *Dare to Submit* (Decklan & Amanda)
Book 3: *Dare to Seduce* (Max & Lucy)

The NY Dares books are more erotic/hotter books.

CONTENTS

Chapter One

The birthday party had wound down, and only family and a few close friends remained in the private room where the celebration had been held. Olivia didn't feel any older, only . . . more jaded. Was it any wonder? It was her twenty-seventh birthday, and she was surrounded by friends and family—if you excluded her wayward father. Of course he hadn't been able to make the party. When had he shown up for anything important in her life?

She leaned against the bar on both elbows and closed her eyes for a few seconds to gather herself before packing up the presents and heading home.

"Happy birthday, Olivia," a familiar masculine voice drawled in her ear. She shivered at the sound, all her senses prickling with awareness as Dylan Rhodes's warm breath heated her skin.

She turned to find him close. Too close, and her pulse picked up speed. Sexy chocolate-brown eyes gazed at her. And his close-cut goatee teased her with its nearness. In her dreams, that sexy goatee felt delicious against her bared flesh.

Jesus, Olivia, get a grip.

"Thanks for coming to the party." Her voice came out too husky for her liking, but Dylan always had this kind of effect on her. He was the travel director with the Miami Thunder, her coworker, and the man she'd lusted after from the day they'd met.

"I'm glad your sister invited me."

She wished Avery hadn't insisted on throwing her a party, but now that it was nearly over, Olivia had had a wonderful time and was grateful her mom and her siblings, half and full, cared enough to attend the event. Friends and coworkers too.

Especially Dylan.

He studied her beneath his hooded gaze. "I wouldn't miss your celebration." He tucked a wayward strand of hair behind her ear, his fingers trailing a path over her cheek in what was a deliberate, lingering touch.

She shivered; her traitorous nipples puckered at his light caress. This was more than the flirting dance they normally did. There was intent in his coffee-colored stare.

She shouldn't be surprised. Until recently, a sense of corporate responsibility had kept them as coworkers only. And then Olivia's brother, Ian, had fallen for his now wife, Riley, and given her a job with the Thunder. Next, her half brother, Alex, had hooked up with his now wife, Madison, and they, too, worked with the team. Ever since, Dylan had stepped up his game. It was like her family's willingness to mix business with pleasure had given him the green light to pursue her. She'd managed to hold out so far, but she knew it was only a matter of time before she gave in.

What are you fighting, Liv? she asked herself. *Too many things,* came the reply. But her quivering insides and the liquid desire pulsing through her veins told her she was going to take the dive and deal with the repercussions later.

"I asked if you wanted your present?" Dylan's voice brought her out of her own head.

She managed a nod, trying not to betray the excitement fluttering inside her. "Sure. I love gifts."

A grin appeared at the corners of his mouth, and he treated her to those irresistible dimples. He was raw, intense, and kept his emotions in check. On simmer, never boiling over.

Although she didn't come from his rougher background, she could relate to the need to hold things close. A father who'd betrayed his entire family in a way only soap operas saw and a first love who had walked away when she needed him most had taught her hard-won lessons. Hell, she was still learning them. Hadn't she believed her father would come? He hadn't even called to say he wouldn't be able to attend. He'd sent a message with her half brother, Alex. She swallowed hard. The confident, tough Olivia people saw on the outside was far different than the sensitive, hurt girl that lived inside her.

She searched and found that outer Olivia now. "So? What do you have for me, hotshot?"

He grasped her hand and pulled her away from the bar, giving her no choice but to follow him, rushing in her heels to keep up.

Her sister, Avery, stared openmouthed as she passed. Olivia's face burned as she realized her entire family was watching Dylan pull her through the lounge area they'd rented for the night and into a darkened hallway.

He came to a halt, turned, and steadied her with strong hands on her waist. "Dylan, what are you—"

He cut her off with a kiss. His lips on hers, hard, demanding, and oh so good. Just as her brain told her this was stupid, he slid his lips over her jawline. She felt that rough beard for the first time, and her mind shut down.

He nipped at her ear, and a low moan reverberated from her throat. "Dylan—"

His hand gripped her hair, tilting her neck back, and his mouth returned to hers. The slight tug on her scalp had the odd effect of arousing her; the moisture dampening her panties was a clear indication she liked this birthday gift and wanted more. Tongues tangled, and she reveled in his taste, a malty flavor from the beer he'd been drinking. No refined scotch for Dylan—he was rough in ways she hadn't been exposed to before him. And she loved it, meeting his demanding kisses with more of her own.

He turned and pushed her against the wall, his hard body aligning with hers. The thick swell of his erection pressed against her belly, and her knees went weak at the thought of what could come next.

He grasped her jaw in one hand and brushed a finger over closed lids. "Open and look at me."

Her eyes fluttered open. Up close, he was even more devastating to look at, pure want and need in his expression. For her.

His hand never left her neck as he gazed into her eyes. "Happy birthday, sunshine." He leaned in and kissed her hard once again. Then he slid a box into her hand, curled her fingers around it tightly, and stepped away.

She glanced down at the gift, dumbfounded. Her body still tingled in all the strategic areas, and her heart was beating a mile a minute. If not for the wall at her back, she would have collapsed to the floor in a heap. But before she could gather her wits, he winked at her. Then he turned and walked away.

Dylan's head spun from that kiss. He'd wanted Olivia for a long time, and this party provided him the perfect opportunity to make it clear things between them were going to change. No more staring at those red-glossed lips and wondering what she tasted like. Now he knew.

He ran his finger over his mouth, coming up with sticky gloss, and he grinned. He'd rendered her speechless—not an easy feat. The sexy vixen now knew where he stood.

So no more using her job as an excuse either. "It's difficult being a female in a male-dominated profession. Getting involved with you will make it look like I can't handle things myself."

He'd called bullshit on that one. Once his assistant, Olivia was now the team's executive director. She was dedicated to her job in a man's world and had to work twice as hard to prove herself as her predecessor had. But she never complained. She was smart, intelligent, and everyone in the industry who met her came to both like and respect her. She'd more than proved herself in their world.

And given her family's propensity to mix business with pleasure . . . yeah. He wasn't buying her reason. She was scared of something. Fine, that he could deal with. He sure as hell didn't do well at relationships either. Which didn't mean he wasn't about to try one with her. They could be good together, given the chance. They shared a mutual passion for football, something that was rare. Dylan ought to know. He'd had enough women try to distract him from his love of the sport.

Added to Olivia's brains and wit, she had a killer body. She was slender with small curves in all the right places, breasts that were made to be held in his palms. He'd had to hold himself back from taking things in that hallway even further. Her waist was made for him to grip hard, and those legs starred in his most heated fantasies. He was a leg man, and he couldn't shake the thought of those long limbs wrapped around him as he slid inside her wet heat.

Now that he knew her sweet taste and her feminine scent, he craved so much more. He intended to have it too.

Dylan headed for the door, only to be stopped by his boss, Olivia's brother.

"I'd like a word," Ian said.

He didn't want to get into his personal choices with Ian, but he respected the man. So he gave him the time. "What's up?"

Ian glanced around. No one was around to overhear. "I realize I'm in no position to judge relationships in the workplace."

Dylan cocked his head. "And?"

"I saw you two in the hallway." Ian shifted on his feet, clearly uncomfortable with the subject.

Dylan had made a scene by pulling Olivia away. He knew Ian was overprotective of his sisters, and since Dylan felt the same way about Callie, his sister, he wouldn't lose his temper now.

But that didn't mean he was opening a vein for the man either. "I don't owe you an explanation."

"The hell you don't. That's my sister you're playing with."

Dylan blew out a long breath. "Who said I'm playing?"

Ian inclined his head, acknowledging Dylan's words. He cleared his throat. "My sister is tough on the outside, but she's . . . more fragile inside," he said, clearly considering his words carefully.

"Your point?" Dylan asked the other man, not wanting information about Olivia from anyone but her.

"Don't play with her head or her heart."

Dylan inclined his head. "I don't intend to."

Ian eyed him through his infamous narrowed gaze, assessing him, causing Dylan to straighten his shoulders and meet his stare head on.

"We good?" Ian finally asked.

"Sure thing." He and Ian had known one another for a long time.

They'd both attended the University of Florida, and Ian had given him a job. They'd run into each other again a few years after graduation. Dylan owed the man, but that didn't mean he had to put what he wanted on hold. Ian would deal with whatever happened. He had no choice, because Dylan wasn't backing down. He was going after Olivia.

The Monday after her party, Olivia grabbed her coffee from the break room and settled into her office at the stadium. She loved her job. Growing up, she'd always wanted to hang with her older brothers, Ian and Scott, both of whom loved football. Although Scott was now a police officer, he never missed a home Thunder game. And since their father's brother, Paul, owned the team, Olivia had been exposed to the sport early. And often.

When Uncle Paul had left the country to travel with his partner, he'd turned the presidency over to Ian, whom he'd groomed for the position. Olivia had graduated college knowing she wanted a position in the front offices. She'd started in PR and moved to travel, learning all she could before being promoted to executive director last year. She loved her job, loved that she worked with some of her family members, and appreciated the players' dedication to the sport and the team and how hard they worked. Coming into work was never a hardship. She considered herself lucky.

Her birthday party had merely reinforced the fact that she was surrounded by people she loved. She'd spent yesterday going through presents and finishing her thank-you notes for each gift. Her sister, Avery, also her apartment-mate, had made fun of her, but at least she didn't have those still on her to-do list.

She settled into her chair and reached into her bag for her eyeglasses. She didn't wear them often, but she'd had a headache today and opted not to use her contacts. But instead of the case, she ended up with the gift box from Dylan in her hand.

She ran her fingers over the velvet covering. Knowing what was inside, her stomach flipped over. This wasn't just a walk-into-a-store-and-pick-out-the-easiest-present kind of gift. This was well thought out and chosen with her in mind. She couldn't bring herself to wear it, and she couldn't stand to leave it home either.

She snapped open the box and looked down at the necklace. The delicate gold pendant of the sun with a sparkling diamond in the center twinkled up at her. Because he called her *sunshine*.

She'd thought it was a lighthearted nickname, not something with more meaning. Even if every time she heard it, her heart fluttered inside her chest. Olivia had no problem admitting she was attracted to Dylan. She was just wary of smooth-talking guys. Oh hell, she was wary of most men— and for what she thought was good reason. *Hello, Daddy*, she thought with frustration. Frustration aimed at herself as well as him because Olivia accepted things as they were. She might be the peacemaker who'd convinced her siblings to, at least outwardly, forgive the father who'd betrayed them, but that didn't mean she didn't have her own issues and internal scars.

As for Dylan, he was a contradiction. From a rough part of Miami, he'd still managed to attend the University of Florida on scholarship. She didn't know much about his past, as he didn't discuss it. She respected that. After all, they weren't friends—they were colleagues. Even if he wanted to be more.

He possessed an edge, one that was apparent even when he wore a suit and juggled the schedules of dozens of players and team management. It was that edge that appealed to her. She liked the guy who'd taken control and dragged her across the room, then kissed her senseless. She was drawn to the man who called her sunshine and gave her this gorgeous necklace. It showcased a softer side of him, and that was the side that scared her. Because she could fall for a man like Dylan. So hard. Which meant she'd be open and vulnerable . . . and experience told her that kind of pain didn't go away easily. She preferred dating men with whom she didn't have a chance of getting in too deep.

She placed the delicate necklace into the box and snapped it closed just as a knock sounded at the door.

She dropped the box onto the desk. "Come in."

The door swung open, and Dylan strode in. *Speak of the devil*, she thought.

Today was casual, no meetings, meaning he wore a pair of black slacks and a white collared shirt open at the neck, revealing a sprinkling of his dark—mouthwatering—hair. His sleeves were rolled up, and she found that even his forearms were muscular and sexy.

"Morning, sunshine." He treated her to a heart-stopping smile.

She swallowed hard. "Good morning."

"Got a minute?" he asked.

She nodded.

He shut the door behind him. "You look sexy in those glasses."

With shaking hands, she pulled them off, suddenly self-conscious.

"You're sexy without them too." He started toward her desk, where his gift sat front and center.

It was too much to hope he wouldn't notice.

The big grin on his face told her she was out of luck.

He sat on the corner of her desk and folded his arms across his chest. "So?" he asked, his knowing gaze on the incriminating box.

Better to face it head on, she decided. "Thank you, Dylan. It's beautiful."

"But you're not wearing it." His lips turned down, and she suddenly felt awful and didn't want to disappoint him or hurt his feelings.

"I was just about to put it on."

His gaze held hers for more than a few seconds before he picked up the velvet box and took out the necklace. "Turn," he said in a gruff voice.

She stood and pivoted around. He stepped up behind her, his body heat already testing her resolve.

"Hair."

She tilted her head forward and raised her long hair off her neck, allowing him to slide the necklace in place and engage the small hook. Instead of him moving away, she suddenly sensed him closer.

His breath fanned her neck, warm air causing a wave of arousal to nearly knock her off her feet.

"What are you—" She couldn't continue, not when his lips skimmed her neck, and her words morphed into more of a moan. His mouth was warm, and he lingered, inhaling her where she stood. Her nipples puckered beneath the silk of her tank, and she grabbed on to the desk for support.

"Do you want to know why I gave this to you? Why I call you sunshine?" His words vibrated against her skin, but he didn't give her a chance to reply. "It's because when I come in to work every morning, seeing you lights up my day."

Oh God. "That's—"

"Corny but true." He grasped her shoulders to keep her steady and rimmed her outer ear with his tongue.

He lit a fuse that ran straight to her core. Suddenly that was all she was aware of, the pulsing of her sex, her damp panties, and her heavy breasts, all three achy and needing his touch more than her next breath.

She wanted to turn, throw herself into his arms, and kiss him for all she was worth. Wrap her legs around his waist and—

A quick knock and her door opened wide. Riley, her sister-in-law, strode in, speaking as she walked. "I wanted to talk to you about—Oh!" She came to a halt. Took in Olivia and Dylan, and a big smile crossed her face. "Looks like I'm interrupting," she said but made no move to leave.

Olivia tried to step away, but Dylan's hands on her arms held her tight.

"Dylan and I were just—umm . . . I mean, Dylan came to discuss the trip to Arizona for the Pro Bowl, didn't you?" she asked in a rush, grasping for a business-related reason for him to be in her office. Not that anything would explain how close they stood or how his lips had been on her neck . . .

Dylan merely looked amused. "Apparently, yes. I'm here to talk about the trip." He stepped away, but his hand dropped, skimming Olivia's lower back. "We can pick this discussion up at lunch," he said.

"Lunch?" she asked, parroting his words because her entire body was still tingling, unable to process what had just happened between them. What would have happened if Riley hadn't barged in?

It wasn't much. It was everything. *Shit.*

"Lunch," he stated. "I'll come get you at noon." He turned to her and winked.

She ignored that in favor of his overbearing push to make plans she hadn't agreed to. "Don't I get a say?" she asked. "What if I already have plans?"

Ignoring Riley's amused grin, Dylan met her gaze. "I gave you a say for the last couple of months. I decided that it's my turn. See you at noon." His fingers glided over her hand as he walked out. "Nice to see you, Riley," he said, disappearing out the door.

"What *was* that? And while you're at it, what was with the caveman routine, dragging you across the room and into the hallway at your party?" Riley—her brother Ian's wife, the team's assistant travel secretary, and Olivia's close friend—settled into the most comfortable extra seat in the office.

Her brown curls hung down her back, her eyes glinting with amusement as she waited for an answer.

Olivia eased back into her chair behind her desk; her awareness of everything around her was heightened. Hell, she was trembling.

"I don't know. We've always flirted, but I thought I made it clear I wasn't going to mix business with . . . anything else." She didn't want to use the word *pleasure* right now. She didn't think her overstimulated hormones could take it.

"Didn't seem like he was listening."

She reached for the pendant around her neck. "He gave me this for my birthday."

Riley rose and leaned in for a good look. "That's gorgeous. Obviously, he's not taking no for an answer. Are you still planning on resisting? And I have to ask, why? He's a great guy and not hard on the eyes either . . . but don't tell your brother I said that." She grinned because they both knew how proprietary Ian could be.

Olivia groaned. "I can't resist him. I don't want to. But he's so intense. Like, all or nothing, and I honestly don't know if I'm ready for that."

"You could keep spending nights home with your TV, or you could go out with a guy who obviously worships you. *Really* difficult choice."

"Oh, that's rich coming from how hard you fought Ian when he went after you."

Riley rubbed her hands together. "Ian scared me because he's so . . . dominant. And you know about my father."

Riley's father had been an abusive, controlling bastard. She'd had good reason to be wary of Ian and his dominating personality. Not that he'd ever hurt her. Worship her was more like it. He'd won her over, but not before she'd almost lost him first.

"I know, but—"

"Just hear me out, okay?" Riley asked.

Because Olivia knew her friend was coming from a good place, she nodded.

"I mistakenly thought trusting Ian would cost me my self-esteem and independence. But you don't have those issues."

"No, but I do have serious trust issues of my own, and you know why."

"Yeah. Your father and his other family. You know I'm well aware of both sides of that issue." Riley was best friends with her half brother Alex.

"So I get why you're wary, but you ought to give Dylan a chance to prove he's one of the good guys."

Olivia forced a smile. There was more to it than just her father. Although she had to admit, he'd been the first man to shatter her faith and continued to do so. She'd thought the sun rose and set on Robert Dare and believed she was his princess, just like he'd always claimed. Problem was, he'd said it when he'd come home from his varied and extended business trips, arms loaded with gifts. And she'd been too young and naïve to know that those presents let him assuage his guilt because he had a mistress and other kids on the side. Kids he gave more time and more of himself to than he ever had to Olivia and her siblings.

Then came Olivia's huge college mistake that merely reinforced the fact that she found it difficult to believe what any man she was involved with claimed.

"Look, I'm sure Dylan is a good guy." A sexy man with dark hair she wanted to run her fingers through and lips she wanted to taste again, Olivia thought.

Riley shrugged. "So go into it with your eyes open. Hot, sweaty sex can be very fulfilling. You don't need to worry about things like relationships and being hurt if you don't invest your heart." Riley met her gaze. "Right?"

A slow smile curled Olivia's mouth. Maybe she *should* stop overthinking things. Dylan wasn't asking for her hand in marriage, God forbid. Then she'd have to dig into her deepest fears and darkest pain. He was just asking for lunch. And probably more, but that kind of more she could handle.

Olivia nodded, finally getting her head in the correct frame of mind to deal with Dylan Rhodes.

Chapter Two

Olivia worked through the morning, but as lunchtime crept up on her, she found herself watching the clock. As much as she'd been fighting it earlier, she was looking forward to going out with Dylan and exploring this thing between them.

Despite the fact that she'd been expecting him—she'd taken a moment to freshen her makeup and fix her hair—when she heard the knock at her door, she nearly jumped out of her seat.

Glasses on or off? she wondered, then quickly pulled them off. "Come in!"

Instead of the man she'd been expecting, her brother strode into the room.

"You're not Dylan." Olivia couldn't hide the disappointment from her voice.

Her usually stoic brother's lips turned up in a grin. "Sorry to disappoint you."

She wouldn't touch that comment. "What brings you by?" And how could she get rid of him before her lunch date showed up?

"Got an emergency with Big," Ian said, speaking of their trouble-prone tight end, Marcus Bigsby, called "Big" by his fans and the media because of his massive size. The guy was six six and two hundred fifty pounds of solid muscle, though still light on his feet.

Big was good-looking, charming, and had developed into an even more phenomenal player in the two years he'd been in Miami. The media and fans loved his oh-shucks attitude. Girls flocked to games to see the golden-haired star player. And the team threw big money his way as part of his renewed contract.

"Uh-oh. What happened this time?"

Ian straightened his tie. "There was a party at his house last night. The neighbors called the cops. When they showed up, his cousin's friends were urinating in the neighbor's fountain."

"Eew." Olivia wrinkled her nose in disgust.

"That's Wendell. Trouble every which way you look at him," Ian muttered.

And therein lay the source of the team's problem with Big. He'd been drafted by the Thunder after his star turn with the Oklahoma Sooners in college. A country boy, he lacked city smarts, didn't know what to do with the money he made, and he was overly susceptible to being used, which often led to stupid choices and negative publicity. Most of which had been instigated by his cousin, Wendell, who had been sent to accompany Marcus to *the big city*, as his family called Miami.

Big was one of the youngest of seven brothers and sisters, and Wendell was only a few years Big's senior, with none of the player's charm or likability. Since he'd been the football star of the Bigsby family until a high school injury had sidelined him, Wendell seemed to think Big owed him a part of his career. He certainly didn't have Big's best interests at heart. He saw dollar signs in his cousin and used him for them. There were rumors that Wendell was involved with the Miami drug scene. But all Big knew was his cousin was family, someone he owed, and someone he naïvely trusted. In other words, Wendell was trouble.

"What's the plan?" Olivia asked her brother.

They'd spoken to Big about the problem before, fined him when appropriate, and tried to counsel him. In fact, they'd enrolled him in the team's program that taught players money management and other skills they'd need for their postfootball career. Her half brother, Alex, had paid special attention to Big, hoping to help him out. Anything to get his head on straight.

Olivia drummed her fingers on the desk as she thought. "As long as Wendell is in the picture, I can't see things changing any time soon."

"That's the plan. Coach Carter is going to tell Big that either Wendell goes home immediately, as in before the Pro Bowl, or he's benching him next season."

Olivia's eyes opened wide. "That will kill him," she murmured.

"Hopefully it'll be the push he needs." Ian glanced at his watch. "Carter's leaving in five. Meet him in the parking lot."

"Wait. What?"

"Big looks up to Coach, but he likes and trusts you. He didn't want to believe Alex when he told him the girl Wendell hooked him up with was a prostitute, but he believed you."

Olivia sighed. "He's such an innocent. He couldn't believe the girl didn't like him for him. I had to explain to him that she was bought and paid for. Because as usual, when Big needed him, Wendell was nowhere to be found."

And Olivia had discovered him in a restaurant near the stadium, waiting for a woman who had no intention of showing up because she hadn't been paid. It had taken her awhile to put things together, but after a word with a couple of his teammates, she'd figured it all out. That had been an awkward conversation, but someone had to have it, and his teammates would have just ribbed him mercilessly.

"Okay, I'll go, but why now?"

"Because Coach wants to go now. Sorry, Liv. We need you for this."

She nodded. "Give me a minute to cancel my plans." She scowled at her brother.

And when he turned his back and walked out, she stuck her tongue out at him behind his back. The babyish gesture didn't make her feel any better, but childhood habits die hard.

It figured. Just when she decided to take Riley's advice and explore her attraction to Dylan, work intruded.

Dylan wasn't happy about his canceled lunch date, but he understood Olivia's reason. He already knew he'd have his hands full with Marcus Bigsby in Arizona for the Pro Bowl trip next week, and if she could help convince the kid to send his cousin away, his job would be much easier. Dylan was only thirty, but when he watched the naïve tight end, he couldn't help but think of him as a kid. Dylan had had more life experience in his teenage years than Marcus had had in his entire life.

Dylan shook his head. He wasn't in the mood to eat in the cafeteria, so he figured he'd go visit his ex. Meg had left a message that she wanted to talk to him, and now was as good a time as any. He could have just called, but he'd heard the tension in her voice, and Meg had a tendency to find trouble. More like she had a tendency toward what she called *bad boys* who brought trouble along with them.

She usually ended up hurt and came crying to him. Sucker that he was for women in distress, beginning with his sister, he usually rode to her rescue.

He walked into the kindergarten class where Meg taught, knowing she had free time for lesson planning. He found her picking up finger paint cans and moving them to a cabinet in the back of the room. Her light-brown hair was pulled into a ponytail, and she hummed as she made her way around the tiny tables she was cleaning.

He cleared his throat, announcing his presence. "Hi, Meg."

"Hi!" She spun around to face him and grinned. Paint-covered hands in the air to keep from getting him dirty, she leaned in and kissed his cheek. "Let me just wash up. What brings you by?"

"Umm, you left a message saying you wanted to talk?"

She glanced at him apologetically. "You didn't have to come in person."

"I know. I had the time."

She rinsed her hands in a tiny sink and finally joined him at her desk. "Half my tuna?" she asked, reaching for a bagged lunch and pulling out a Ziploc bag.

He nodded and shrugged. "Can't say it's the lunch I had planned, but why not?" They settled into chairs and sat in silence, sharing her homemade sandwich.

High school sweethearts, he and Meg had broken up to go to college. When they'd reconnected years later, they'd tried to pick up where they'd left off, but it hadn't worked, and they'd ended up agreeing that the old spark was gone. However, they made for good friends, and it worked for him.

"I have got to find something else to make for lunch. I'm tired of tuna." Meg crumbled her foil up and tossed it into the trash.

"Okay, now that lunch is over, what's wrong?"

She rose and strode over to a pile of construction paper and began hanging up her students' drawings, not answering him right away. A clue all in itself.

"Is it Mike?" he asked of her live-in boyfriend. "What did that asshole do now?"

She didn't turn around to face him as she spoke. "A sudden boys' weekend in Vegas. With money he never seems to have for us," she said, sounding defeated.

Dylan hated how that lazy bastard used her. "I thought he worked weekends. Isn't he the foreman on a construction crew? How does he have free time to go party?"

She dipped her head. "Yeah. About the job . . . He said he prefers doing hands-on work and stepped down from that position."

Dylan grunted. "In other words, he was demoted or fired."

"I don't know that for sure."

"Did you ask him not to go?"

She nodded. "He blew up at me. Said he needed a break and to back off. Then he apologized and promised to make it up to me when he got back."

Dylan stood and came up beside her. "Why do you keep picking these losers? Don't you know you deserve better?" he asked.

The conversation was reminiscent of words he'd used with his mother . . . before she'd packed up and left them for good.

Meg turned to him, eyes watery, and he pushed the old memories aside.

"You were the last decent guy I picked. Sometimes I think I'm trying to find a better you." She laughed, grabbed a tissue from her desk, and wiped her eyes. "Why couldn't we be good *together* together?" she asked.

He thought of a certain brunette with knowing eyes and a wide smile and knew there was no one else he wanted to be with. "We grew up, Meggie," he said, using his old nickname for her. One nobody used anymore.

She nodded. "I know. Kissing you now would be like kissing my brother. If I had one," she said, wrinkling her nose.

He more than felt the same way. "Mike's taking advantage of your generosity, not to mention your pocketbook." The guy didn't pay rent, rarely kicked in for food or anything else, and now he'd likely lost his job but was off to party in Vegas. None of which meant things would be changing any time soon. "Kick the bastard out the minute he gets home. And be more careful with your picks next time," he said as sternly but as gently as he could.

She nodded, but he knew it would never be that easy. With Meg, drama seemed to follow.

"Thanks for coming over. You always know how to give me that shove in the right direction." She leaned in and hugged him tight, her cheek rubbing against his.

The way she lingered told him more than anything how hard a time she was having. "Hang in there."

"I will. Talk to you soon. And thanks again."

"I'm used to being your sounding board."

"More like my knight in shining armor, but don't worry. I intend to find one who really belongs to me one day."

He shook his head and laughed before heading back to the stadium.

Dylan had a lot of work to do, but he stopped by Olivia's office on his return. Their lunch might have been canceled, but he wasn't finished with her. Not by a long shot.

He knocked, because she deserved a little heads-up, and let himself in before she could reply—because why give her too much time to pull her defenses together? He caught her at her desk, glasses on, in front of the computer screen.

She glanced up, and he got what he wanted, an unbridled look at her initial reaction. Startled pleasure before she wiped her expression clear. "Dylan. What brings you by?"

He started slowly. "How'd your meeting with Big go?"

She pinched her nose and sighed, her concern for the player all too obvious. "He really doesn't understand that Wendell is bad for him. It's sad, really. Marcus is one of those players who got through college because the teachers looked the other way with his grades." She shook her head. "So added to lack of a solid education, he's got no street smarts at all. There's not a bit of slyness in him."

"Because they all went to Wendell," Dylan muttered.

Olivia nodded, her eyes sad. "Yeah. But between Coach's bad cop and my good cop routine, we convinced him he needs to stand on his own and get rid of his cousin."

"He understands what's at stake?"

She spread her hands out on the desk. "He should. We made it clear."

"So no more prostitutes he believes are real dates coming in and stealing the Rolex he neglected to put somewhere safe?"

She managed a smile at that memory.

"And no more arrests when Wendell and his buddies start a fight at a club?" he continued. Big had a history of following his cousin into trouble strictly out of loyalty.

"You know what?" Olivia asked. "I believe that without Wendell around, he'll have more time to focus on his training, his game, and on Alex and Madison's career and lifestyle programs. He has the chance to really learn something productive about how to save money for the future and how to live his life during and after his time playing football."

She finished her passionate speech, dark eyes flashing with the intensity of her beliefs. Her cheeks flushed, and of course, she had to lick those sexy red lips. Dylan couldn't help but smile.

"What's that grin for?" she asked.

"You really care for Big. It's sweet."

She blushed at his compliment. "I just want him to succeed at more than football."

He settled a hip against her desk. "This is so much more than a job for you, isn't it?"

She shrugged. "I grew up wanting to be like Ian and, later, Alex, after I met him. Not as in I wanted to play, but I wanted to be a part of the sport. Honestly, when I was younger, I think learning the game and tagging along after my older brother gave me something to focus on when my dad was away traveling."

He nodded, listening, wanting to hear more.

"And then when I found out about Dad's other family . . . football was something that had nothing to do with him." She turned away, obviously embarrassed at the admission.

But he was grateful for the reveal and the insight into what made her tick.

"What about you? What made you get into the sport?" she asked before he'd even formulated a reply to her story.

He swallowed a groan. He should have realized she'd want to know something deep about him.

He cleared his throat. "I guess you could say football was a good distraction for me too. Kept me out of the house and gave me a goal and potential security for the future." And that's all he wanted to get into at the moment. "Now you canceled our lunch today. How about you make it up to me?"

She wrinkled her nose, giving her an adorably kissable look. "What exactly did you have in mind?"

What he wanted and what he would get were two different things. He wanted to slide between her silken thighs and fuck her until she couldn't see straight. But that was his cock talking. His brain, what little gray matter worked, understood patience was his friend.

"Join me for dinner tonight."

She propped her chin on one elbow, meeting his gaze. "You know, you're getting awfully bossy."

He grinned. "And does that turn you on?"

Her breath hitched at the question. He didn't need a better invitation. He strode behind her desk and swung her chair around to face him, then leaned down, bracing his hands on the arms of her seat. Beautiful deep-blue eyes stared up at him.

"What do you want from me?" she asked.

Everything, he thought. "A chance," he said instead.

She parted her lips, and he had no trouble taking advantage of the opportunity, covering her mouth with his. She stiffened in surprise, but when he nipped at her lower lip, she parted instantly, a soft moan bubbling up from her throat. The sound went straight to his already aching, ready cock.

He glided his tongue over the spot he'd tasted, soothing her before delving deeper, tasting all of her. And she was right there with him, her soft tongue tangling with his. Back and forth, he glided around the wet recesses of her mouth, groaning his approval each time she met him with equal fervor. And though he wanted nothing more than to take this to its inevitable conclusion, she deserved a slow seduction. But Jesus, the things this woman could do to him with no thought or effort.

He breathed in her floral scent and continued kissing her for all he was worth before finally lifting his head. "So? Dinner?"

She blinked at him, her soft gaze refocusing as awareness returned. She shook her head and wrinkled her nose in obvious distaste. "You smell different."

"What?" he asked, offended and confused.

Olivia pushed at his shoulders, needing space.

"What the hell?"

Olivia breathed in deep and narrowed her gaze, seriously annoyed with herself for letting one little nip of her lip suck her in and make her forget the change she'd noticed the minute Dylan had come close.

"You smell like another woman's perfume. I realized it the second you kissed me. Then you overwhelmed me with that kiss . . . but what the hell, Dylan?"

He muttered a curse. "It's not what it looks like." Dylan, obviously upset, met her gaze. "I went to see an ex-girlfriend. We're *friends*."

Yeah, Olivia thought. She'd heard all that before. Like when she'd questioned how much time Jeff, her college boyfriend, had spent with his teaching assistant. *We're friends*. And when she'd caught them huddled together . . . *It's not what it seems*. And when she'd gone to tell him that she was pregnant, he'd been with said assistant, legs tangled, clothes off . . . They obviously hadn't been doing homework. She'd learned to ask questions much earlier and to look further than what she wanted to believe.

Olivia blew out a long breath. *Listen and don't jump to conclusions*, she warned herself, but even years later, it was hard.

"Look, we haven't really been together since high school. She's been having some boyfriend problems and asked if we could talk, so when you canceled lunch, I went over there." He shrugged. "She works at an elementary school nearby. She teaches kindergarten," he added, unnecessarily, in Olivia's mind.

"I see." She bit down on her lower lip, worrying it with her teeth.

"I can tell by your tone of voice that you don't see. At all."

She folded her arms across her chest, using any defensive mechanism she could to keep him out. Because he'd gotten to her with that kiss. He'd slid his tongue into her mouth, and she'd forgotten all about that heavy floral fragrance she'd noticed when he'd leaned in—before overwhelming her completely.

"How much of an ex is she?" she asked. "I mean, while you're trying to pursue me and convince me to give you a chance, just how good a friend is this woman you went to see?"

He held her gaze, telling her either he was a pro at lying or he had nothing to hide.

He rubbed at his goatee. "Like I said, we've known each other since high school. We went out back then, split up for college, and when we both moved back here, we thought about getting back together, but it just . . . wasn't there anymore. So we're friends. And that's it."

She blew out a long breath. "Right."

"What's that mean?"

"It means I've heard that 'we're just friends' line before."

"Hell, Olivia, do you really think I could kiss you that way and still want someone else?"

She blinked and shook her head, forcing herself to be in the present and not the past. She really gave his words thought and blew out a long breath.

"I try not to be the kind of woman who jumps to conclusions." Although her life experience had given her good reason to do just that.

"Then don't." He stepped forward, more hesitantly than he'd done earlier.

She nodded, knowing he was right. But that didn't mean she liked what had just happened. Or how it made her feel. She had no right to be jealous about Dylan or anyone in his life, but the fact remained that she had been. And that meant what she felt for him, or *could* feel, was more than just casual. The very reason she'd been ignoring his push for more between them. Because the potential for getting serious about him was there. And that heightened the possibility of being hurt.

"So . . . dinner tonight?" he asked.

She shook her head slowly. "I'm busy," she lied, forcing the rejection out of the same mouth that wanted to kiss him again.

He eyed her through a narrowed, knowing gaze. "Yeah, right. I'll be over around seven. I'll bring the food. See you then." He turned and headed for the door.

"Dylan!"

"Yes?" He turned and leaned against the doorframe, looking too damned sexy and appealing, making it hard for her to resist him.

She could still feel the scruff from his goatee on the sensitive skin around her mouth. She lifted her fingers to touch her lips, caught herself, and dropped her hand.

"You can't just tell me what you're going to do and expect me to do it."

He cocked his head to one side. "No, under ordinary circumstances, I couldn't. But you want me. You wouldn't respond to me so beautifully otherwise. True?"

She opened her mouth, then shut it again.

He nodded, seeming pleased with her nonanswer. "See? One of us has to be brave in this situation, and it's obviously not going to be you. Someone has to push. And that someone is me. I'll see you tonight."

And then he was gone.

Chapter Three

Olivia rushed home from work and hurried to shower and get ready before Dylan arrived. She loosely braided her hair, letting it fall over one shoulder, added minimal but necessary makeup, and changed into the fifth outfit she'd tried on.

She hadn't planned on putting so much angst into getting ready for Dylan, but she couldn't decide on what was appropriate. The jeans showed she didn't care, which just wasn't true. Same for her cute, favorite pair of sweats. A skirt was too much like what she wore in the office, and she couldn't feel flirty and sexy in one. She finally chose an easy sundress with thin straps and a floaty feel to the body that hit her midcalf. Casual but pretty. She liked it.

Finally ready with a few minutes to spare, Olivia walked into the kitchen to find her sister standing at the sink, finishing up rinsing off a glass.

Avery turned, looked Olivia over, and grinned. "You look hot."

"Thanks. And you look comfortable," Olivia said of her sister's baggy gray sweats and a light-blue T-shirt. She'd pulled her dark hair into a messy ponytail.

"Well, I think you chose well." Avery, who loved picking out clothes and makeup, looked Olivia over again, approval in her gaze.

"I just picked out something casual."

"You mean if I went into your closet, there wouldn't be a pile of tried-on clothing on the floor?" she asked knowingly.

Olivia ignored her and opened the refrigerator, looking to see what kind of white wine they had chilling. She pulled out a Chardonnay.

When she turned around, she found her sister hadn't disappeared. She still stood there grinning like a fool.

"Okay, out with it. What's put that goofy smile on your face?"

Avery laughed. "I was just thinking about how you told me Dylan insisted he was coming over for dinner and ran roughshod over you when you said no. Almost makes me want to applaud him for not putting up with your shit."

"What shit would that be?" Olivia asked. "I mean, really. Name one woman who thinks her man smelling like another female is okay."

"Aha! You called Dylan *your man.*"

She rolled her eyes. "That was just a figure of speech. And you didn't answer the question."

Avery grew more serious, her smile gone now. "No sane woman would put up with it."

They both knew their mother's experience clouded their judgment in all things.

"So what's he bringing for dinner?" Avery asked.

"Why do you care? You won't be here, remember?"

Because when she'd come home and explained her evening plans, she'd asked Avery if she'd disappear for a little while. Being a good sister, she'd agreed.

"I know. I just want to be here when he arrives. You know, shake his hand, give him the evil eye, and make sure he brings you home on time. Or in this case, leaves at a decent hour." She wiggled her eyebrows at her own joke.

"You're insane."

She had always been the more lighthearted, easier-going sister. Even after being tapped as a bone marrow transplant for the half sister they'd just learned they had, Avery had never lost her sense of humor. Olivia admired that in her sister. She didn't let life get to her as much as Olivia did. No, that wasn't right. Avery didn't *show* it as much as Olivia. She hadn't built her walls as high, even though they both had good reason.

"I want the best for you, and I happen to like Dylan." Avery looked Olivia over from head to toe. "Can I give you some sisterly advice?"

"On dating? You're younger than me."

Avery rolled her eyes. "I'm also wiser. Look, go for it. Have fun for once in your life."

Had Avery been talking to Riley about her? Both of them seemed to feel the same way. Even though the last time Olivia had let loose and had fun, when she hadn't overthought, she'd paid a huge price.

"Don't go there. Just don't." Avery touched her hand, bringing her out of her memories. "Enjoy tonight. Enjoy Dylan. I'm sleeping at Ian and Riley's. I'm going to babysit my niece so the tired parents can spend time alone. In other words, don't wait up. Or expect me back. I'll see you after work tomorrow."

As if on cue, a knock sounded at the door. "Perfect timing!" Avery picked up her packed duffle on her way to the door. "Do you want to make a grand entrance?"

Olivia gritted her teeth. "Go away, little sister."

Avery grinned and opened the door. "Dylan! What a nice surprise. Oh! Let me take some of those."

Before Avery could drop her bag, Olivia rushed forward. "I've got them." She took some of the bags out of Dylan's arms, allowing her sister to finally head out the door.

Leaving her alone with Dylan. He'd changed from his work clothes of pressed pants and collared shirt into a pair of worn jeans and a navy polo tee. She caught a glimpse of his fine ass as he walked to her kitchen with his armful of bags.

He placed them on the counter and turned. "How's it going, sunshine?"

Her hand immediately went to the pendant, and he grinned. "It's going."

"You look gorgeous."

She felt herself blush. "Thank you. You look pretty good yourself." His arms were muscular from time in the gym, and his skin was tanned a warm golden color. His shirt revealed a sexy hint of hair on his chest and that same tanned flesh. Her mouth watered, and she wondered what he'd taste like if she gave him a slow lick from the end of the V in his shirt up the strong column of his neck.

She shivered at the thought.

"You okay?" He'd caught her staring, and a knowing smirk lifted his lips.

God. She nodded. "What's for dinner?"

"Arturo's. The best Italian around." He proceeded to pull out a variety of tins with aromas that smelled heavenly, transferring them to dishes she provided.

They worked well together in the kitchen and settled in to eat. The meal passed quickly, and they drank a good amount of the Chardonnay she'd served. They discussed work and some of the changes to his job since Riley, his assistant, had cut back after the birth of her daughter. They talked about football and how frustrated the entire team and management were that they'd fumbled and lost the final game that would have led them to the Super Bowl.

"I am so full," she said when she couldn't eat another bite. She looked at the table with all the remaining food.

He'd brought them so many options—chicken parm and pasta dishes, some that she knew the names of, others that were chef's specials. There was no way they could eat everything, so she'd settled for sampling each. "Everything was delicious, Dylan. Thank you."

"My pleasure." He smiled, and the simple act lit her up inside.

Her stomach rolled like a teenager with her first crush. And her sex pulsed, a distinct reminder that she was a woman sitting across from an extremely attractive man who wanted her—and was willing to pull out all the stops to get his way. She was drawn to him on so many levels.

He was smart. He did his job well. He loved football. And he'd set his sights on her. She was attracted to him beyond reason, and this extravagant meal had simply shown her another side of his persistent personality. To her surprise, she couldn't say she minded being the recipient of all this attention. But the idea of a relationship between them still scared her. More like the idea of a relationship that would ultimately end did.

She picked up one of the dishes still overloaded with food. "I'll wrap these up for you so you can take them home and freeze them," she said, rising from her seat. She might not be able to escape from her desire for Dylan, but she could keep busy and get out of her own head.

"You keep the leftovers. You can defrost one after a long day." He winked at her and stood, then proceeded to help her clean up and freeze the leftovers.

He was making it very difficult not to enjoy and appreciate his thoughtfulness.

"Thanks for helping me. You really didn't have to."

He shrugged. "I wanted to." He leaned against the now-closed dishwasher.

"Well, your mother must have raised you right."

"She didn't raise me at all," he bit out, the harsh tone of voice catching her off guard. He'd been so easygoing all night.

She swallowed hard. "I'm sorry. I didn't mean to hit a nerve."

He shook his head and swore under his breath. "You had no way of knowing. She took off on us right after my sister, Callie, graduated high school. I still had another two years left. But she was barely around before that. My sister and I pretty much made do on our own."

Wow. That was unexpected. And so opposite of how she'd been raised. In a big, fancy house with everything she'd ever wanted. A father who ran a hotel empire and traveled constantly—for business, she'd thought—but she'd had her mother and her siblings to support her. Olivia was so close to her own mother that she couldn't imagine getting through the hard parts of her life without her mother's sage advice and wisdom.

She glanced at him from beneath her lashes. His expression had shuttered, his jaw tensed. Her heart hurt for the little boy who'd clearly been forced to *make do.*

"What about your father?" she asked hesitantly.

"Didn't know him. My mother used to say she thought Callie and I had different fathers, and from the looks of us, I'd say she was right."

"She didn't know for sure?" Olivia asked, her voice rising with her shock and outrage.

He raised one shoulder. "Men came and went." The disgust in his voice was obvious.

"How did you . . . well, end up being you? You got a scholarship and now a great job." With no adult in the house who'd cared enough to give him direction or love?

He shrugged, but his discomfort was obvious. "Callie picked up the slack around the apartment, and I worked as soon as I was old enough to get a job. Paid under the table delivering groceries, but it was something. She made sure I did my homework, and I wanted to succeed and make money so I could take care of her for a change."

"Oh, Dylan. You two are lucky to have had each other."

"Now that I agree with." He shook his head and, with the motion, seemed to rid himself of the memories and the mood. "So how about dessert?"

She wasn't about to argue the change of subject. "What do you have?"

"Cannoli." He walked over to the refrigerator and grabbed the pastry box he'd put inside.

"My favorite dessert in the entire world! Now I'm going to have to make room. And definitely fit in a workout tomorrow."

He grunted at that. "What a coincidence. Cannoli is my favorite dessert too."

"Coffee?" she asked, gesturing to the one-cup brewer.

He shook his head. "No thanks."

She opened the cabinet to pull out plates. "Leave it. Cannoli is best from the box."

She shrugged. "If you say so."

They returned to their seats around the table, the open box of Italian pastries in the center. Dylan still seemed quiet, something she attributed to the conversation about his childhood. She decided a change of subject was in order.

"So you're flying to Arizona this Wednesday," she said. The Pro Bowl was a week from this Sunday.

"I am." His eyes lit up at the thought.

The Thunder had four players voted in this year, Marcus Bigsby included. Those playing usually flew in a week or so early and spent quality time at the resort. The guys with families savored the opportunity for a pregame vacation. Arriving on Wednesday would give Dylan a chance to adjust to the time zone change before the planned activities began on Friday night. And he'd be available to monitor player interviews earlier in the day.

He nodded. "I'll have time to enjoy myself a little before the insanity starts."

"Starting with a five-hour flight. But it is Arizona, you lucky dog."

"Have you ever been there?" he asked.

She shook her head. "Maybe someday. I heard the spas in both Phoenix and Scottsdale are amazing."

"I know I'd love to see you in a bikini," he said all too frankly, taking her right back to being on the fine edge of desire.

With all the serious talk about his past, she'd forgotten he was determined to both charm and seduce her. The molten look in his eyes, the heat and need all for her, was a heady feeling.

"Dylan—"

"Come here." He crooked his finger her way.

Frowning, she stood and walked over. He'd turned his chair so he was facing her as she approached. As soon as she came within reach, he pulled her onto his lap.

She squirmed uncomfortably but stilled when she felt his erection beneath her thighs.

"Good idea," he said in a roughened voice. He smoothed her hair off her cheek, and his fingers lingered, tracing the line of her jaw, gliding down her neck and up again. Arousal became a living, breathing thing inside her.

"Now stop fighting me and let's talk," he said, back to taking charge.

Really? How did he expect her to concentrate with his hard length pressing into her, causing her sex to pulse and swell?

She swallowed hard. She had two choices. Ask him to leave or go along with what he had planned.

Not much of a choice.

"Okay. What do you want to talk about?"

He continued to leisurely caress her cheek. "I'm sure you've dated before."

"Of course I have!"

He laughed at her indignant tone, causing her to flush with embarrassment. Her cheeks were probably flaming. "Your point?" she asked.

"Do you give every man who wants to be with you this hard a time?"

She blew out a long breath, understanding now where he was going with this conversation. "No."

"Why me then?" Dylan asked, but in his gut, he already knew the answer. He just wanted to hear Olivia admit what was going on inside her head so they could deal with it and put it behind them, once and for all. If she stopped fighting herself, there was so much for them to explore.

He'd spent too much time imagining the hollows and curves of her body, her wet heat drenching his cock, tasting her sweet essence. Jerking off to those thoughts and more. He needed to experience reality, and to do that, he had to quell her misgivings, whatever they were. That had been his plan for the evening, not the detour into his past. The revelations had been like slicing open a vein, but if the insight into what had made him who he was helped ease her fears, it was worth it.

So he'd bled for her. He hoped she was willing to dig as hard, and as deep, for him.

"Well?" he asked, stroking her cheek and enjoying the feel of her soft skin against his hand.

"You scare me," she said on a soft breath of air. Yet with the admission, she turned her face into his hand, seeking more of his touch. He doubted she was even aware of her actions, but arousal rushed through him at the trust that little action implied.

The last thing he wanted to do was frighten her. "Why do I scare you?" he asked. He stopped touching her skin and picked up her thick braid and tickled her shoulder with the end strands.

"It's complicated. We know each other already. We have an obvious connection. And it's intense."

He grinned. "Yes, it is."

"One of us could get hurt," she said, looking at him with wide eyes.

And she was afraid that someone would be her. Interesting. "Life's a risk," he murmured.

"I've lived mine lately without taking too many of those."

He paused in thought. "Let me catch you if you fall, okay?"

She visibly swallowed hard. "But we work together. Things can get awkward if we don't work out."

He couldn't argue that point. But he wasn't about to let it stop him either. "You're the one with the job security, sunshine. If things go wrong, your brother could kick me out on my ass. And I'm willing to take the risk."

"You don't know me," she said.

"But I'm going to." He'd had enough. "You admitted there's something real between us. You're a strong woman who competes in a man's world, and yet you're willing to run without seeing how good we can be? That's not the Olivia I've seen so far. She wouldn't bolt at the first sign of trouble."

She narrowed her gaze. "You're right." But he could tell she didn't like admitting it.

"So we can agree that when you told me you wouldn't go out with me because you didn't want anyone to think you're weak, that was bullshit?"

"Yes," she said, even more ungraciously.

He laughed at the mulish expression on her face. She didn't like being pushed hard, and he admired that. "Good. So now that we've gotten all those things out of the way, anything else you want to tell me? Anything else I don't know about?"

She blinked at him and started to wriggle in an attempt to climb off his lap. Running away again. He grasped her arms to hold her in place. "I'm going to take that as a yes, there's more I don't know."

"But—"

He placed a hand over her lips, and she stilled. "But I'm not going to ask you about it now. I need to earn that right. Agreed?"

She nodded slowly, the tension easing out of her in slow beats. "So what now?" she asked.

With a grin, he reached for a pastry and held it up for her to bite.

The man was dangerous, Olivia thought. From the hard thighs beneath hers to the delicious treats he offered, to the temptation *he* presented, she was done for. And so what? She was so tired of second-guessing what felt so good. He wasn't worried, so why should she be?

She grinned back at him, opened her mouth, and let him place the cannoli between her lips. She bit down, and the creamy ricotta squirted inside her mouth.

"Mmm." She moaned loudly at the sweet taste that exploded on her tongue, and the cream ended up all over the outside of her mouth. "Oh God." Embarrassed, she looked around for a napkin, but there was none. They'd cleaned up too well.

"Let me," he said in a husky voice. And he licked her lips, curled his tongue, and sucked the pastry cream into his mouth.

A lick here, a taste there, another nibble on her lower lip. Her belly twisted with arousal, and she clenched her thighs together as his cleanup of dessert turned into a tongue-tangling, lip-clashing kiss.

He grasped the back of her head in one hand and held her firmly against him, his mouth doing seductive, wicked things to hers. Long, slow laps around the inside of her mouth that ended with him sucking on her tongue until she writhed in his lap, her sex damp and pulsing with the need to get closer. She wanted that thick erection pressed against the most sensitive part of her, but her legs dangled sideways over his, and all she could do was moan and want.

He tugged at her hair and tipped her head back, those talented lips now trailing a warm path down her neck until he reached her collarbone. He remained there, tasting her, nibbling with his tongue and teeth. She was certain he'd leave a mark, especially when he nipped hard enough to hurt, a pain that soon blossomed into intense pleasure. And more wetness between her thighs.

"God." She pushed off him, grasped his shoulders, swung her legs around, and settled herself back on his lap, her arms wrapped around his neck. Looking into his lust-filled eyes, she shifted until they were groin to groin, her sex nestled against his.

"Take what you need, sunshine." He raised his hips, and a wave of pure desire washed over her, all-encompassing and so good.

She threaded her fingers through his longish hair and kissed him hard, loving how he tasted and how he clearly appreciated the act of just making out and not rushing to the final act. He also wasn't selfish, and as she rocked into him, her body lit up with need.

"Lift up."

She did, and he pulled her dress up so he could slip his hand beneath the hem. His big hands cupped her breasts. Warm and solid, the pressure felt so good. She arched her back, pressing her aching nipples into his palms. All the while, her hips rocked back and forth against the swell in his jeans.

"Gotta get rid of all this material."

Without warning, he yanked her dress over her head, and she raised her arms to help him. He tossed the offending garment onto the floor, leaving her in only a skimpy push-up bra—because the girls weren't all that big alone—and a barely there pair of thong underwear.

He splayed his hands over her waist and eased her backward so he could look his fill. A blush rushed to her cheeks. She'd never been all that thrilled with her lean body, but from the sheer approval in his gaze, he didn't see her the same way.

"Damn, baby, those are gorgeous breasts."

She blinked in surprise. "The bra's pretty incredible." She didn't want him to be disappointed later.

He cocked an eyebrow. "Really? Because I'm kinda liking *them.*" He leaned down and pressed a light kiss to each mound overflowing its cup.

She trembled at his awe and quivered when his warm breath hit her skin.

He reached behind her and, with more dexterity than she wanted to think about, unhooked her bra and sent it the way of her dress.

Nearly nude while he was clothed, she felt completely wanton and a lot embarrassed.

"Stop thinking and go back to feeling." He tweaked her nipple, and she moaned.

His big hands came back to her hips and encouraged her to begin rocking against him once more. Those glorious waves began to fill her again, and her embarrassment fled. Once she established a rhythm, he left her to it and refocused on her breasts. Each hand played with her at once, his fingers rubbing and tweaking, rolling and playing with her nipples. The alternate stinging pain and soothing touches combined to set her on fire.

She locked her hands around his neck and rolled her hips, amazed at the intensity of the sensations. A part of her understood it was this man—his touch, his interest, his awe in her body—that enabled her to let go. A distant part that would have let the emotional fear back in if she weren't so far gone.

But she couldn't stop reaching for the climax that was so close, she could practically feel it. Sounds she'd never made before escaped her throat as she ground herself down on his cock. Suddenly his warm hand reached down, his fingers sliding beneath her underwear to glide over her clit.

Sensation shot through her, and she whimpered out loud. "Dylan, please."

"Anything you want, sunshine." He glided his fingers back and forth over her pussy, obviously letting her needy sounds guide him, because finally he settled where she needed him most.

"How's this?" he asked, pinching her clit, then releasing, finding a quick and steady rhythm that had her catapulting headlong into a blinding orgasm.

"Oh God, Dylan. I'm coming!" She squeezed her legs around him as everything inside her coiled from a tiny ball into a starburst of feeling, taking her higher than she'd ever been. She rode against him, aftershocks pummeling her body until she collapsed, her head against his shoulder, his strong arms around her back.

She'd barely caught her breath when she felt him move.

"Up you go." He rose with her in his arms. "Your bed-room?" he ground out.

She lifted her head and pointed to the right side of the apartment. "First door down the hall."

Next thing she knew, he laid her on her bed and began a quick strip out of his clothes. She'd come back to herself enough to realize she'd come, yes, but she was still aching and empty. She wanted him inside her, and if she felt so needy, she could only imagine how frustrated he must be.

She had a quick glimpse of his naked body—tanned, mus-cular, gorgeous—before he came over her, bracing both arms on either side of her head. "Watching you come? That was the hottest thing ever."

She grinned. "Yeah?"

"Yeah." He arched his hips, and his thick cock did a slow glide over her sensitive flesh.

She doubted she'd come again, but she wanted to feel him filling her up and watch as he took his pleasure this time.

He gritted his teeth and groaned. "Shit."

"What?"

"I didn't want to be presumptuous. I didn't bring protec-tion. Figured if I did, you'd throw me the hell out." He dipped his head, his frustration clear. And so cute.

"I have a few in my drawer. It's not like I need them or use them all the time, but I mean, I just always figured it's better to be prepared than not . . . and I'm rambling."

Dylan knew he pretty much had blue balls at this point, but he managed a laugh anyway. "I'm not going to complain that you can solve the problem."

But he was damned glad Olivia didn't make it a habit of need-ing them. That old double standard was hell, but it did apply. He wasn't overly sexually active either, but he'd definitely had his share of women. None since he'd set his sights on Olivia and decided to give her time to adjust to the idea. But did it make him a jackass that he didn't want to think of her needing condoms with other guys? Probably. Not that he gave a shit.

"Where are they?" he asked.

"My drawer." She pointed to the nightstand. "But I'll get it." She tried to crawl out from under him, but he was too happy with her hot little body beneath his. "Don't move."

He reached for the drawer, pulled it open, and the first thing he grabbed wasn't a condom but a bright-pink vibrator.

"And that's why *I* wanted to get it. Reach farther back," she muttered.

An adorable flush stained her cheeks, in addition to the abrasions from his beard. He liked his marks on her, he thought. And he intended to leave more.

He held up the piece of equipment and grinned. "We'll use this later," he said and tossed it to the side. He found the condoms, opened one, and rolled it over his aching cock.

"You still ready for me?" He reached down and slid a finger over her bare pussy and through her slick wetness, easing it inside. He nearly exploded from the feel of her tight inner walls gripping his fingers. "Mmm. You are."

He glanced down. Big, desire-filled eyes gazed up at him as her hips arched, trying to hold his finger inside her.

He chuckled at her eagerness. "No way, sunshine. Next time you come, it's going to be around my cock, not my finger."

She blushed as he poised at her entrance.

Taking the cue from both the condom comments and how tight she'd been, he held on to his desire to slam into her. "Has it been a long time for you?" he asked.

She bit down on her lower lip and nodded. "Awhile."

He was pleased as hell with that answer. "We'll go slow," he said and nudged the head of his cock inside. Holy shit, she was tight. His balls were so heavy they hurt, and he needed to thrust.

A low moan escaped her lips, and he counted to five in his head, then, still holding back, he pulled out and slid back in farther. "Still with me?"

"Oh yeah." She arched up, taking him a fraction more. "I'm not fragile, Dylan. I won't break."

But he didn't want to hurt her and have her end up with regrets either. He eased out, and when she bent her knees, he thrust all the way in deep.

She raised her legs and wrapped them around his waist. That was all he needed to lose it. He pumped into her with slow, steady thrusts she met with soft groans that told him he was hitting all the right spots. Lord knew she was doing it for him.

"Damn, sunshine, you are so fucking wet and hot around me." He accentuated his words with a deep thrust.

"Harder," she said, digging her fingers into his shoulders. "I swear you won't hurt me."

The sting of her fingernails and the plea in her words had him slamming into her hard and fast. All sense of time and place disappeared. The sound of the headboard hitting the wall and the creak of the bed echoed in his ears along with her cries and his own guttural groans.

He kissed her quickly because he needed to breathe, and his climax was rushing at him fast. "Not coming without you," he told her, pushing up on his hands and angling his next thrust so he hit a spot that had her screaming out loud.

"Oh God, that's it, Dylan. I'm so close."

He grunted and slammed into her again, aiming for the same angle as he rolled his pelvis over her sex. Her inner walls gripped him, her nails dug into his skin, and she cried out his name as she came. Her climax around his cock had him swearing and his balls rising and tightening, his own orgasm hitting without warning. Pleasure like he'd never felt before ripped through him, and he kept jerking his hips, gliding into her until he collapsed on top of her.

He wondered how he was still breathing. Because he'd nearly blacked out from the pure ecstasy he'd found inside her body. Somehow he managed to roll off before he hurt her, shocked when she groaned as he slipped out of her body.

"God, I think I passed out," she muttered. "It was that good."

He burst out laughing at her description. "Gotta say, it was spectacular." *Beyond*, he thought as he rid himself of the condom, wrapping it in a tissue from her nightstand and putting it aside to dispose of later.

He pulled her into his arms and waited for his breathing to return to normal. "I didn't hurt you, did I?"

"God no," she murmured.

"Okay then."

"Okay."

She rolled onto her back, and he propped himself up so he could look into her eyes. "Are you leaving?" she asked.

Hell no, he thought. "You thinking of kicking me out?"

She pursed her lips as if she were actually considering it, and his damned heart nearly stopped in his chest.

"I didn't let you break down my walls so you could eat, sleep, and leave."

The wariness was back in her gaze, and he didn't know if she was more worried that he'd leave . . . or that he might actually want to stay.

"I don't plan on going anywhere."

"Okay then." She nibbled on her lower lip. "Want to shower?"

He grinned. "You mean, do I want to clean up so we can get all dirty again? You bet." Without giving her a chance to think again, he rose and pulled her out of bed, letting her lead the way to the bathroom.

He stared at the slender column of her back and that perfect ass, unable to believe he'd made this much progress. He should have pushed the point much sooner. Because sliding into the warm cushion of her body felt right in more ways than sex felt good. Like she was made to fit around him. It'd been better than he'd imagined, and he'd jerked off to thoughts of her often. But this wasn't jerking off. It wasn't just sex. It was something good and well worth the effort he'd had to put into pursuing.

Chapter Four

Olivia's phone alarm woke her up for work as usual. She fumbled a bit before managing to shut it off, then rolled back, her arm hitting a solid object. Last night came back to her in vivid detail, her body acknowledging every erotic act flashing through her mind.

Suddenly she was hot and bothered, her body achy and warm. Sex, more sex, a hot shower in which they'd soaped each other up and rinsed each other off, only to indulge in yet more sex beneath the running water. Of course, that meant they'd created a wet trail to her bedroom so they could get to the condoms, but it had been worth it.

After rinsing off again under cool water, they'd fallen into bed, and apparently they'd both crashed hard. Because now it was morning.

She couldn't remember the last time she'd woken up with a man in her bed. Then again, she couldn't remember the last time any guy had pursued her with such single-minded determination either.

She didn't feel like she'd given in. She felt like they'd started something that, just maybe, she could let herself believe in. A big male arm reached out and snagged her waist. Dylan dragged her beneath him, and she realized he was already erect. Apparently there was truth to the rumors that men woke up that way. She let out an inadvertent giggle.

"What's so funny?" He propped himself up so as not to squish her.

"Nothing. I'm just amusing myself."

He smoothed her eyebrows with his fingertips, and she sighed at the light stroke. Something she realized about Dylan—he was a toucher. Something she was learning about herself—she liked to be touched by him.

"And you won't share?" he asked.

She grinned. "Nope." Some things a girl had to keep to herself.

She felt lighter this morning than she had in a while. Fighting their attraction, fighting *him*, had been wearing on her. She looked him over. In the early morning, he had sexy scruff around his goatee, and his heavy-lidded eyes seemed to devour her, and moisture trickled down her naked thighs. Acting on impulse, she reached for his erection and glided her hand up and down the velvety length.

He groaned and arched into her grip. "Don't tease me," he warned her.

"Not teasing," she promised and tossed the covers off them, easing down his body until she was facing that massive part of him that was apparently wide awake and ready for her. "We have to get to work, so we'll have to move it along," she said, then swiped her tongue over the head.

He let out a rough groan. "Oh man. You do not have to—"

"I want to." She cut him off with her words and punctuated her statement by pulling him into her mouth. He tasted like musk and man with a hint of salty flavor, and she hummed her approval, causing him to thrust his hips up, sending his length deeper.

Her eyes watered, but she wasn't giving up until she'd accomplished her goal, making him feel as good as he'd made her feel all last night.

"Sorry, baby," he said, tangling his fingers in her hair and tugging the long strands as she began to lick him slowly and steadily.

She slid her lips up and down his shaft, taking time to tease the sensitive spot beneath the tip before gliding down once more.

Soon he was pumping his hips up and down in time to her rhythm. She added her hands to the base, tightening her grip around his moist length, adding pressure along with the suction caused by her mouth.

He groaned hard and tugged at her hair. The entire experience had her aroused and on edge, her sex heavy and wet, the need to finish him in her mouth warring with the very real need to slide down on top of him and ride him to completion.

She moaned at the thought, and the vibrations triggered his release. He spilled his essence inside her mouth as she swallowed quickly, taking every drop he gave until he was spent. She released him gently, laid her head against his chest, and caught her breath.

"I like waking up with you."

Warmth spread through her. *Ditto*, she thought, not ready to reveal her feelings as easily as he did.

"C'mere, sunshine." He pulled her up and covered her mouth with his, ignoring where it had been and kissing her for all he was worth.

And as she'd learned, the man could kiss. She purred, rolling her hips against him, causing him to break their connection on a chuckle.

"Don't worry. I'm going to take care of you too."

"Good to know." Actually he'd proven himself such a generous lover last night, she'd had no doubt he'd soothe the building ache.

He flipped her over and began to slide down, his greedy eyes devouring her, making every negative thought she'd had about her body flee in the wake of his approval.

His hand gripped her thighs. "Spread for me."

Her breath hitched, and she did as he asked, leaving her open and exposed.

"Who needs breakfast when I have this?" He slid one finger over her sex, parting her lips, then dipped his head and licked her. One long swipe of his tongue, followed by a satisfied moan.

She trembled, her entire body arching at the intimate touch. "God, Dylan."

He ignored her, suckling her clit, and she started a slow climb to ecstasy. He ate at her like a starving man, and she loved the sensations he created as he played with her body.

She writhed beneath him, so close, so fast that she began reaching for the climax just out of reach. That's when he slowed down, and the languorous feelings drained away. "No!"

"Yes." He chuckled and teased her clit with the tip of his tongue. "Delayed gratification only makes it better."

She couldn't reply, not when he delicately teased that most sensitive part of her in a way that had her lost and on a fine edge of need. The slightest bit of pressure would set her off, but he seemed determined not to provide it.

Instead, he slid one finger inside her as he kept up that light, teasing touch.

She began to pant, to arch her hips, to grab at the sheets and beg. "Dylan, please!"

"Please what? I want to hear it."

A toucher and a talker. She nearly wept at the intensity of the desire that teased her but wouldn't take her over. "Please make me come. Please!"

He added another finger, spreading her wider, pumping them in and out, *still* not letting her fall over. "You're killing me," she practically wailed.

"I'm going to give you the best orgasm you've ever had," he promised, and if the building pressure was any indication, he was right. She just didn't know how much more teasing she could take.

"Ready?" he asked, his breath warm and tantalizing against her sex.

She whimpered in reply. He'd reduced her to a needy mass of nerve endings and raw emotion. Then suddenly, he curved his fingers inside her, pressing in one spot, then another, hitting exactly the right place, and she moaned, the tremors beginning in earnest. He added his mouth, sucking hard at her clit while thrusting with his fingers, and she screamed. Everything inside her burst open, shooting spiraling heat, and warmth blindsided her in an explosive climax that seemed to go on and on, endlessly perfect.

And just as she came down, she realized he'd grabbed a condom and thrust inside her quickly. Hard. And deep. He kept driving into her, somehow finding that already sensitized spot that immediately sent her spiraling a second time.

She didn't know when she came back to herself. How long had they been lying there catching their breath? She rolled her head and looked at him. A wondrous smile met hers.

Yeah. She got that. *Pretty incredible*, she thought.

"Don't move. I'll be right back."

He rose from the bed and strode out of the room still naked. She couldn't tear her gaze from his strong body, the lean line of his spine, and the grooves above his ass. She hoped her sister didn't choose that moment to arrive home.

She laughed at the thought. Avery had wanted her to go for it. To have fun. And she had. A whole lot of fun that made up for a long stretch of deprivation. But even she knew it was more. She and Dylan clicked so well, it was scary.

And just like it always did when she let herself go and be happy, the inevitable comparisons began to form in her head. Was this what her mother had felt when she'd met her father? How long before she'd known things weren't what they seemed? Because Alex wasn't that much younger than Ian, which meant her father had been cheating almost from the start. Or maybe her mom hadn't known. After all, Olivia had been clueless when Jeff was fooling around with his teaching assistant right under her nose. She shook her head. It was hard to dispel the ridiculous thoughts and comparisons. She needed to put the past behind her if she wanted to enjoy her life.

And Dylan seemed to be giving her a lot to enjoy.

Dylan stuck around for breakfast with Olivia and Avery, who'd announced her arrival by yelling at them for leaving her clothes around the dining room table. Dylan had laughed. Olivia had been mortified. But Avery had brought muffins, Olivia had made coffee, and they'd eaten quickly. Dylan then pulled Olivia to the front door, leaving her with a long, deep kiss intended to let her know how much he'd enjoyed their night.

He arrived at work—separately from Olivia, at her insistence, not his, because he didn't care who knew they were together. No sooner did he settle into his desk than they were called into an emergency meeting.

With the Pro Bowl a little over a week away, Ian wanted a meeting. After Big's latest episode, caught, of course, by TMZ, Dylan understood the man wanted to be sure all bases were covered. Although the Pro Bowl was mostly an individual endeavor, the players still represented their teams. Which left Dylan with a lot of responsibility on the trip. And no time to deal with distractions.

But as he settled into his seat at the conference table, was his focus on team image? The players? The travel schedule? Hell no. It was on the woman who'd opened her body to him last night. Her rich laughter echoed around the room as she laughed at something Riley said, the husky sound thickening his blood, and he clenched his pen tighter in his hand.

He narrowed his gaze just as she glanced from beneath her eyelashes and looked directly at him. He raised an eyebrow, and she grinned, pursing those luscious lips that had been wrapped around his cock this morning, before immediately returning to the paperwork in front of her. Beneath the table, he pressed his hand against his thickening erection, cursing her effect on him when he couldn't do anything about it.

"Okay, people. Let's talk." And that was Ian's way of calling this meeting to order from the head of the table.

To his right was Riley, then Olivia; to his left, Coach Carter and the PR people who worried over every misstep.

"Dylan? You first." Ian sat down, ceding the floor.

Dylan nodded. "The hotel is set. The Montelucia Resort and Spa in Scottsdale has our reservations."

"Double-checked and confirmed," Riley, his assistant, added.

"I'm meeting with the attending players this afternoon, along with the PR team." He inclined his head their way. "We'll go over the ground rules, the planned interviews, and the possible unplanned ones. There won't be any problems."

"I should hope not," Ian said. "Liv, you're going."

"Wait . . . what?" Olivia asked, obviously caught off guard.

"Coach told me there was no way he'd have gotten through to Big without your influence, so in case there's trouble, I want you nearby."

She opened her mouth and closed it again, as Dylan did his best not to grin. Apparently, fate was looking down on him, because he and Liv were headed to a desert oasis for a week of business, yes, but plenty of private time too. Not that Ian knew he was facilitating Dylan's agenda.

"Problem?" Ian asked his sister.

A sudden grin lifted her lips. "Scottsdale, Arizona, for a week? No, no problem."

Ian ignored her excitement and moved on. "Carter, you're there for backup."

The other man, an ex-MVP himself, now forty-five and a star coach the Thunder was lucky to have, merely nodded. "Always planned to be there."

Olivia tapped her pen against the table. "Dylan, what time is your meeting?" she asked, meeting his gaze. Those Dare sibling eyes, a deep indigo fringed by thick black lashes, stared back at him.

Those same eyes had looked at him with wonder last night seconds before just one of many explosive orgasms had hit her hard. He swallowed a curse and shifted in his seat, but his discomfort remained. "Meeting's at three in the locker room," he told Olivia.

She nodded. "I'll join you there. Big needs to know we mean business."

The next thirty minutes continued with the PR people laying out the plans for next week and their proposed spin on Big's latest antics. Finally, the long meeting ended.

"Everyone set?" Ian asked, glancing around the table.

Murmurs of assent arose, and everyone grabbed their folders and things and filed out, heading to their offices to work.

Dylan waited, knowing Olivia had to walk past him to exit. As she approached, he caught a whiff of her perfume, a scent now permanently emblazoned on his brain.

"Liv—"

"Dylan." She strode up to him, her folders pressed against her chest, pushing up those fabulous breasts he'd felt intimately against his bare chest. "What can I do for you?" she asked.

"Aah, that's a loaded question, Ms. Dare."

A lovely flush stained her cheeks, but a knowing smirk pulled at her lips because they shared a secret. An intimacy no one knew about. And he had to admit it was a rush. He had to shove his hands into his front pants pockets in order to keep them off her.

"I guess you're going to spend the weekend getting ready and packed?"

She nodded. "Good thing we live in Florida. I already have the type of clothing I'll need."

He leaned in close. "I was hoping there'd be plenty of times you wouldn't need much in the way of clothing."

She sucked in a shallow breath. "You're bad, Mr. Rhodes."

"I can't wait to show you just how bad I can be."

At eight a.m. the morning of their departure for Arizona, Olivia dragged her suitcase behind her through the terminal in Miami Airport. She wore a light-blue pantsuit, knowing that as soon as she hit the hotel in Phoenix, she would change into more casual clothing; but for now, she represented the team. She made it through check-in and security, then stopped to buy herself a bottle of water before heading to the gate and settling in. Typical, she was punctual to a fault, early when she flew, and she was the only person from the team at the gate, so she settled in with her iPad and headphones.

She wasn't sure how much time had passed when she felt a tap on her shoulder. She glanced up to see Marcus Bigsby standing over her. If she'd been outdoors, he'd be blocking her sunlight completely. He was that large.

She pulled her earphones from her ears and glanced up at him. "Hey, Marcus. Fancy meeting you here."

"Good morning, Miss Olivia."

She smiled at his formality. He could be so proper sometimes, so troublesome others. "It's bright and early, that's for sure. You all set for Phoenix?"

He settled his large frame into an empty seat across from her. "I guess."

She frowned. "It's your third Pro Bowl. Aren't you excited?"

"Yeah. But my mama's mad at me for sending Wendell home. She thinks I need family by my side."

"You don't need a keeper. You just need to trust yourself a little more." *And Wendell a little less*, but she didn't say that out loud.

"You believe that?"

She nodded. "I do." For all the self-confidence he had on the field, he was sadly lacking in it in other areas. But his teammates liked him and had taken him under their wings, and things could only get better from him from here on in.

"Big, my man!" Glenn Sanders, the Thunder's running back, made his arrival. At five feet ten inches, small by football standards, the blond-haired player strode over, and the two men exchanged handshakes. "It's a good morning to fly!" Glenn said with a grin before turning to her. "Hey there, Ms. Dare."

She smiled at him. "Looks like you're a morning person."

He laughed and grabbed the seat next to Marcus. Grateful the other man had a diversion from thinking about his cousin, Olivia returned to her reading, only to be distracted a few minutes later by a familiar masculine scent.

"Miss me?" Dylan asked as he smoothly slid into the empty seat beside her.

She shook her head. "Too busy picking out clothes and packing," she lied as she pretended to continue reading a magazine on her tablet. In reality, she couldn't focus on anything but the man beside her and how just his very presence had lit up her day.

"You really know how to hurt a man's feelings." He leaned in close, nuzzled his nose against her neck, breathing in deep. "You smell good."

So did he. She closed her eyes and inhaled his musky scent once more before wriggling to the far side of her chair. "We don't want the players noticing us." She turned and met his amused gaze.

"I don't think they'd care."

Neither did she, but there was something to be said for acting professional. "We need to set a good example for them."

Dylan stared at her long and hard for a minute before turning to the other men. "Anyone want some coffee?" he asked.

Marcus, Glenn, and Sawyer, who'd joined them, shook their heads. "No thanks," came a chorus.

"Well, I do." He rose to his feet. "Come with me." He grasped her hand and pulled her to her feet.

"Bossy much?" she muttered. "Hang on." She slid her hand from his. She placed her iPad into her travel bag and pulled out her small purse. "Guys, watch my things?"

The players nodded.

Dylan gestured for her to walk ahead of him. She couldn't help but take in his outfit, the black slacks and cream shirt that gave him a sophisticated, sexy air. Her awareness of him shot up several more notches, making her desire to keep their relationship a secret even more difficult.

No sooner had she started walking down the wide hall than he slid an arm around her waist and pulled her into an empty gate area, not stopping until they reached a corner hidden from view.

"What are you doing?" she asked, breathless.

"Getting you alone so I can have my morning kiss." He braced one hand over her head and leaned in, pressing his lips against hers.

"Mmm," she practically purred, not denying how much she wanted the same thing.

He swept his tongue into her mouth, and her entire body came alive, the lingering hint of mint and Dylan packing a powerful punch. She slid her tongue against his, and the needy feelings she'd been suppressing all weekend burst forth, making her feel awake and alive. One big hand gripped her waist; the other tugged on her long braid, sending pulsing sensations directly to her sex as his mouth devoured hers.

"Now *that's* a good morning," he said as he broke the kiss.

"Yeah. It is." She slid her tongue over her lips, and his heated gaze followed the motion.

"Tease."

She grinned.

"Before I'm tempted to start something I can't finish here and now, how about that coffee?" he asked.

She nodded. "Sounds good." She could use a spike of caffeine before getting on the plane for the long trip.

He walked with his hand against the small of her back, a possessive gesture she found she liked. A lot. They got in a short line at Starbucks, and when it came time to order, he asked for a grande dark coffee for himself before turning her way. "Soy latte?" he asked.

She blinked in surprise.

"You worked with me long enough," he reminded her. "And when it comes to you, I pay attention."

She was ridiculously flattered by that one comment. The man knew all the right things to do and say. Could he really be as genuine as he looked? Was any man?

Drinks in hand, they headed back for their gate and resettled into their seats. An announcement reminded them they'd be boarding as soon as the plane had been cleaned from the previous flight, and she was eager to get under way.

She pulled out her phone and texted her sister, telling her she'd talk to her from Arizona, sent another text to Ian because he liked to worry, and sent one to her mom.

"Check in with everyone?" Dylan asked, an amused smile on his handsome face.

"Some of them."

He leaned close on one arm. "What's it like? Growing up in such a large family?"

She thought about it before answering. "Well, the good thing is, you're never alone. The bad thing? You're never alone," she said, laughing.

"Must be cool though."

"It had its moments."

"And your mom was great, right?"

She nodded. "She's a strong lady."

"Lucky," he said, his tone darkening. He was obviously thinking about his own mother and her shortcomings.

What could she say to a man who'd never really had either parent? At least Olivia and her siblings had had their mother, Emma.

"You had your sister," she said, searching for something positive to say.

He inclined his head. "And she's great. But the holidays were small. And hard without a lot of money to buy her gifts."

She sighed. The grass was never really greener. Nobody had everything, which was something she'd come to understand.

"On the other hand, we got everything money could buy. And that was the problem. My father was trying to buy us. I think he believed that if we weren't lacking in material things, we wouldn't care as much that he wasn't around."

"And did you? Care?"

"A lot," she whispered, her voice catching. "I mean, do you know how many Christmas mornings we opened presents with Mom because we thought Dad was working, only to find out later that he was with his mistress and her family?" She blinked back tears she didn't often let fall. She'd accepted the situation a long time ago. "Did you happen to notice who was missing from my party?"

Dylan frowned. "Did he say why?"

"Sent a message with Alex. Called afterward. But it's always the same story."

"And yet you don't resent Alex or the rest of your half siblings?"

She swallowed hard. "It's hard to explain why I don't. Ian more than resented our father for a long time. He probably still does. But Avery and I . . . We were presented with the situation when our half sister Sienna was seriously ill. She would have died without bone marrow. I couldn't help but feel for sorry for all the kids. And when Avery tested positive, I refused to leave her side at the hospital. I got to know them too. So the resentment got pushed back in favor of the reality of new siblings and a really sick girl." She shrugged, having explained her crazy past as best she could.

Had it scarred her? Without a doubt, but he didn't need to know just how much her father's betrayal had wrecked her ability to trust men. Even she hadn't realized it until Jeff's unfaithfulness at the worst possible time had driven the point home.

She glanced down, startled to realize Dylan had begun to stroke the top of her hand with his calloused fingers, offering comfort and understanding.

He cleared his throat. "Parents can do a real number on their kids." He shook his head, obviously referring to both of their parents. "I'm going to throw out my cup. Can I take yours?"

"Thanks." She handed him her empty cup, grateful he'd decided to let the subject drop. It had been an unexpectedly heavy conversation, revealing parts of her psyche that were still wounded. Even if *he* wasn't aware of the fact, she'd reminded herself, she hated that those old feelings were intruding on what should be a fun time with Dylan.

She stood, ready to stretch her legs, shake off the past, and take advantage of the coming week of sun, fun, work, and yes, one extremely sexy man who seemed intent on showering her with attention. That was something she intended to enjoy.

"Flight 882 Miami to Phoenix is ready for boarding. We will begin with our first-class passengers," the disjointed voice said over the sound system just as Dylan rejoined her.

"Ready?"

"Can't wait." Her anticipation and excitement returned.

He bent and picked up the handle of his carry-on just as his cell phone rang.

"I'll grab this as we head over to the gate."

She shrugged and started to walk beside him as he put the phone to his ear.

"Hey, Meg. Just getting ready to board. Anything important?"

His ex-girlfriend, calling him as he boarded a plane to leave town? Seriously? That quickly, her good mood evaporated. It wasn't that she didn't believe men and women could be just friends . . . or maybe she didn't believe it, after all. Especially a man and a woman who'd once been in an intimate relationship. Didn't Meg have any girlfriends she could call with her problems?

"Okay, look, you can either pack up his shit or wait till he decides to get his lazy ass home from Vegas and have him do it himself, but it's time."

Great, so he was encouraging her to break up with her boyfriend. Olivia hated where her thoughts were going at the moment, but she couldn't seem to help herself.

When they reached the attendant in charge of boarding, he said, "I'll talk to you from Phoenix." Pause. "Yeah. Take care. Bye."

Olivia gritted her teeth and handed the woman her boarding pass, had it scanned, and marched down the gateway.

"Liv, wait up!" Dylan called after her.

She slowed, and he caught up to her. "Sorry about that. Meg's having some problems with her boyfriend."

She raised her eyebrows. "And she turns to you to solve them? That's sweet." She stepped onto the plane, hurt and annoyed for no good reason—and for every good reason. She couldn't decide which.

So she settled herself into her seat, aware of Dylan's worried stare as he took his seat beside her. But she had nothing to offer him, no response. Instead, she asked an attendant for a pillow, accepted a blanket, curled up, and went to sleep.

Chapter Five

Dylan knew he'd fucked up the minute he'd said Meg's name out loud. *He* knew his feelings for Meg were purely platonic, but he was beginning to wonder if Olivia believed what he'd told her.

He frowned. He didn't like to think she didn't take him at his word. Then again, if she'd gotten a phone call from an ex right before boarding, not long after he'd smelled the other man's cologne on her shirt, he wouldn't be a bundle of sane understanding either.

"Shit."

They'd ascended a little while ago, and Olivia had slept through takeoff. He had a feeling she was avoiding him and any conversation about Meg.

He ran a hand through his hair and glanced over at his sleeping beauty. Olivia's profile had softened. Her long, loose braid fell over one shoulder, and occasionally, soft little sounds escaped her throat, making him smile.

He had no doubt his feelings for her were different than any he'd ever had before. From the moment they'd been introduced and he'd shaken her hand, he'd felt as if he'd been sucker-punched. When he'd discovered she could talk football plays, he'd fallen even more under her spell. She'd been involved with someone back then, and he should have made a move then.

He was finished with distance now.

Olivia awoke with a stiff neck, her head tipped to one side, the pillow beneath her hard. She opened her eyes, took in the backs of the seats in front of her, and realized she was on the plane and she'd laid her head on Dylan's shoulder in her sleep.

She wanted to jump up, but the crick in her neck prevented quick movement. "Oww," she said as she slowly straightened her head.

"Hey," Dylan said. "Are you okay?"

"My neck hurts. Awkward sleeping position." She forced herself to turn and face him. "I'm sorry I ended up sleeping on you."

"I'm not."

She blew out a long breath. "Dylan—"

"Livvy, I'm going to tell you something, and I want you to hear me."

Uh-oh. She curled her leg beneath her.

"It's about Meg."

She swallowed hard, her mouth dry. "You don't owe me an explanation." While pretending to sleep, before she'd actually dozed off, she'd done some thinking. She might be jealous of this ex-girlfriend—she'd be lying if she didn't admit to that—but she and Dylan had merely slept together. They didn't owe each other anything. This was a fun affair, and she had to treat it as such.

"It's okay. Once again, I owe you an apology." She hoped to stay any long descriptions of his relationship with the woman. "I don't have any right to question your friendships."

"You don't?"

She shook her head. "No. I mean we're having an affair. Sex, fun, and now some sunshine added in. It's all good."

He narrowed his gaze. "Oh really?"

"Yes. I'm going to have to watch that tendency of mine to forget my place."

"Your place." He sounded as if she'd lost her mind, so she rushed to explain.

She nodded again. "We're not in a relationship, so it won't happen again." She held up her hand. "I promise."

He shook his head. "Did you hit your head in your sleep? Is my shoulder that hard?"

"What are you talking about?"

"I'm thinking you must have amnesia. Because I distinctly remember telling you we're going to see where this thing takes us. That's more than an affair in my book."

Panic immediately set in. She felt too much for this man in a very short time. She'd been down that route before. Young, careless, and suddenly pregnant, while her boyfriend was carrying on behind her back and she ignored the signs.

Because she'd wanted to mean something to someone so badly. She'd wanted the man in her life to love her and give her the security that had been ripped away from her when her father's other family had been revealed. She and Avery were no longer his special princesses; they shared that role with Sienna, his other daughter. His other children who didn't get guilt-induced gifts; they got *him*, his presence at school events and holidays, not work-related excuses.

So she'd put her hopes on her first serious boyfriend, and not only had he cheated on her, but when she'd told him she was pregnant, he'd reacted as if she'd managed the feat alone. An immaculate conception. He'd wanted nothing to do with her or the baby.

"Olivia, are you okay?" Dylan waved a hand in front of her face. "You're pale, and you aren't answering me."

She blinked and resettled herself in the present. "I'm okay. Sorry. I just . . ." She searched for a plausible explanation for her mental lapse and decided on the truth. "I have baggage, Dylan. It's not obvious, and not a lot of people know about it, but I think the notion of you being in contact with your ex put me back in that place."

He nodded, his dark eyes wide and understanding. "We already established the fact that there are things I don't know. And I wouldn't push you. You'll tell me when you're ready."

She ran her tongue over her dry lips. "So you're a patient man."

He tugged on her braid. "In some ways and about some things, yes." Pulling her braid, he brought her face within millimeters of his. "And in other ways, about other things, not so much."

He licked at her lips, and she melted into him.

"There you go. Just go with the flow. The rest will work itself out, okay?"

"I'm working on it," she promised him as much as herself.

He parted his lips for a delicious kiss, one that made her forget every insecurity and issue that had been running through her brain. Until a catcall-like whistle interrupted them.

Dylan turned, and they both glanced up to see Marcus standing there with a grin on his face, making a thumbs-up sign with one hand.

"Busted," the tight end said with a grin.

Olivia felt herself blush, knowing their secret was out. She wasn't really worried about anyone knowing; she just wanted her professional reputation intact. But now that Big knew, it wouldn't be long until the rest of the team did too. Which she had a hunch would give Dylan license to act on public displays of affection. And that didn't bother her as much as she would have thought.

Olivia waited in line at the Montelucia Resort and Spa to check in. The airport had been overflowing with visitors excited for the upcoming game, and the hotel was the same, making check-in a nightmare.

Dylan had stayed back with the driver to make sure the bags were tagged appropriately, and she appreciated a break from the constant awareness she felt when he was near. The heat of the desert had nothing on the heat Dylan had generated in the seat next to her.

The four-and-a-half-hour flight had been long, his leg constantly brushing against hers—and staying there. He liked to play with her hair and spent a lot of time idly tugging on her braid, running the ends over her cheek and trailing the long tail under his nose and inhaling her scent.

She waved a hand in front of her face. She told herself the heat coming in from the open lobby was killing her, but she knew better. She'd been thinking about Dylan. Fantasizing, really. It had become a bad habit. But no man had ever been so hyperfocused on her before. He made her the center of his attention, and there was a part of her still starved for affection. That was the part she distrusted, because it led her to do stupid things and ignore important signs.

"Luggage is all taken care of," Dylan said, joining her and taking her breath away with just a look. From his dark hair to the goatee she so adored, to the toned body, thanks to working out at the stadium gym, the man was sex personified.

It didn't help that he was smart, good at his job, and had a way with the players and upper management, getting what he needed without demanding or bullying. She'd always been a sucker for a smart, handsome guy, and Dylan was the whole package.

"Good. Thanks for handling our bags."

"Line moving?" he asked.

"A little." There were still a few people ahead of them.

"Where are the players?" she asked, glancing around but not catching sight of them.

"Signing autographs. One of the benefits of having the Pro Bowl in Hawaii, like we usually do, was more privacy. That changed this year. But they seem to like the attention. Only Maddox and his wife and baby will want more privacy," he said of their married player, who had arrived earlier today with his family.

She nodded. "He travels with security when his kids are with him. It'll be fine."

Her cell rang and she answered. "Hello?"

"Livvy! How's Arizona?" her younger sister, Avery, asked.

"Beautiful. Hot. And too damned crowded," she muttered, but the line ahead of her had dwindled to two people, thank goodness.

"How was the flight? Did you give in to Dylan and let him make you a member of the Mile-High Club?" her sister asked.

Olivia glanced at the man in question and took a discreet step away. God forbid he overheard her loudmouthed sister or read the look of desire on her face at the very thought of what Avery had suggested. "Don't you have something better to do than to bug me?" she asked, unable not to laugh.

Her sister sighed loudly into the telephone for effect. "Come on. You're already doing it. Now you're in a luxury hotel with hot tubs and swimming pools and all the amenities. It's like . . . kismet. Fate. At the very least, it's—"

"Business." Olivia stated the obvious.

"I was going to say romantic."

That too. But she wasn't going to give her sister the satisfaction of agreeing.

"Next!" The man at the front desk signaled for Olivia to step forward.

"I have to go check in," Olivia said, relieved to be able to disconnect with Avery and the topic of conversation.

"Okay, but remember what the shrink said. You can't let your past define your future."

The shrink she'd seen once, when the depth of her grief and despair had been overwhelming. She hadn't returned because talking about losing the baby she'd finally wrapped her head around wanting seemed futile. Reliving the experience in that sterile office had been too hard. The reality had been painful enough, and she lived with it still.

"Gotta go, Avery," she said as she stepped forward.

"Let loose! Have fun! At least have more sex!" her sister called out in a rush just as Olivia ended the call.

"Anything important?" Dylan asked, a grin on his handsome face.

"No. Just Avery being Avery."

They stepped up to the desk.

"How can I help you?" the dark-haired clerk asked.

She leaned on the counter and met his smile with one of her own. "I'm Olivia Dare."

Dylan eased in beside her. "Dylan Rhodes." He leaned close, and his arm brushed hers.

Electricity shot up her skin.

"So are you two here on vacation?" the clerk asked. "Honeymoon maybe?"

Dylan grasped Olivia's hand and held it tightly on the counter. Warmth pervaded her system, and she tried unsuccessfully to pull free.

"Unfortunately I haven't been successful in convincing her to marry me, but I'm not giving up." He turned to Olivia and treated her to a panty-melting grin. The darned fantasy took hold.

She drew a deep breath, shot him a warning look, and yanked harder, freeing herself from his grip. "He's kidding. We're here on business."

The clerk glanced back and forth between them, obviously confused. "What were the last names again?" he asked.

"Dare and Rhodes," Dylan said first. "With the Miami Thunder. Corporate reservation," he said, now all business. "And we're checking in our players. The whole reservation is under the Miami Thunder organization."

The other man looked down and began tapping his keyboard. "Ah, yes. I have five suites reserved on the same floor."

"You mean six. Six suites," Olivia said.

"Bigsby, Sanders, Flynn, Maddox, and Rhodes," he said, reading the names off the monitor.

"Maddox is already here, yes?"

The clerk did some more typing and nodded. "Yes. He checked in earlier."

"Flynn will be here later," Dylan said. "But you're missing Dare. Olivia Dare. I confirmed these reservations myself."

Some more clicking followed. "I'm sorry, but I only have the five. And we're booked solid." A concerned and contrite look spread over his face.

"But my team is in this hotel. I need to be here too."

"Liv, you can have my room." Dylan placed a hand on her shoulder. The skin-to-skin contact sent her senses soaring, and her anxiety level about being separated from the team sparked even higher.

"Can you find me something in another hotel?" Dylan asked.

She shook her head. He was the travel director. He needed to be here, take care of the scheduling and other important matters. "You can't switch hotels." Although she appreciated the offer.

"I really would like to help you out, but most hotels are booked solid for the Pro Bowl. It's going to be difficult finding you other accommodations," the clerk said with regret. "I don't know how this happened." He went back to his computer and tried to find what Olivia knew would be impossible. An empty room.

"The only thing I can say is that Mr. Rhodes has a suite. Of course, it's a king-size bed and an outer room with a couch, but we can send up a rollaway." The young clerk shrugged, clearly uncomfortable.

Join the club, buddy, Olivia thought and pinched the bridge of her nose, well aware a headache was building. It was one thing to have an affair with the man. But without her own room, a place to escape to? No breathing room? Constant togetherness? She didn't know if she could handle it. She also knew she didn't have a choice.

"I'll take the rollaway," she murmured. "If you don't mind sharing."

He shot her a disbelieving look. "We'll discuss sleeping arrangements later," Dylan said, then handed his corporate credit card to the clerk.

Olivia pushed out a breath and managed a nod. They both knew that once they were alone in that suite, neither of them would end up on the cot.

A bellman escorted them to the Full Camelback Mountain View Suite. The oversized living room led into a beautiful master bedroom, and the terrace did, indeed, overlook the majestic mountains, giving them a glorious view.

"We can split the drawers," Dylan said easily. "You go first and choose your space. I'll put my stuff in the bathroom."

"Thanks." Olivia unpacked her things quickly, making sure to leave room for him even if she had to squish all her items together in both the drawers and the closet. His unpacking took a lot less time. And as he hung his last pants and shirts next to her sundresses and evening wear, a pang hit her squarely in the chest. One she couldn't identify and didn't want to examine too closely.

She escaped to the bathroom. He'd chosen the left side of the sink with the smaller counter space, leaving her more room. He was a gentleman, one whose sister had taught him what it meant to live with a woman, she thought, appreciating him. As she laid out her toiletries, the intimacy of the situation wasn't lost on her.

Neither was a truth she hadn't wanted to face. Since losing both Jeff and her baby, she'd convinced herself life was easier and better alone. Jeff might have been a college boyfriend, but they'd fallen into the habit of sleeping over and leaving their things in each other's rooms. She'd never let anyone close since. She'd had affairs with men she liked but none she'd call relationships. She already felt more for Dylan than she had for any man in her life, and now they were truly sharing space. She shivered and pushed the thought aside.

She walked out of the bathroom to find Dylan grinning at her from one side of the king-size bed. He'd changed into a pair of swim trunks, his gorgeous chest and muscles on display.

"The bed is comfortable." He patted the free side of the mattress. "Tell me you aren't considering calling for the rollaway."

She wasn't surprised he asked. She was taken aback by the hint of uncertainty she saw in his gaze. For the first time, she realized it wasn't all about her. *He* didn't want to be rejected.

She stepped over to the bed and crawled on, stretching out beside him. "No cot for me. I'm sleeping with you."

In the blink of an eye, she was flat on her back, Dylan's big body looming over her. He smelled so good. And just the tease of his strength and the notion that only their clothing kept him from filling her deeply made all other worrisome thoughts flee from her mind.

"I'm glad you chose me over some lumpy cot." He brushed his lips over hers and rolled off, levering himself to a sitting position, then rose to his feet.

Well, that was a tease, she thought. "What are you doing?"

"We flew in early and have a couple of days to settle, so I'm going to head on out to the pool. You coming?"

She nodded. She stood and stepped to the window, looking down at the pool and the many guest chairs beckoning.

She turned and was stopped short by the sight of Dylan's bare chest. She hadn't forgotten he had a heart-stoppingly gorgeous body, but seeing it again had her wanting to tackle him back onto the bed and roll around until his big, strong body dominated hers.

"Something wrong?" he asked, a knowing grin on his face.

"Not a thing. I just need to get my bathing suit." Suddenly she knew just how to get back at him for arousing her body and walking away. She swung around and headed to find a bathing suit and cover-up in the chest drawer.

She had a few options to choose from. Knowing she would be poolside with the players and their families, she'd brought mostly bikinis that covered an appropriate amount of skin. But she also had one string bikini she knew she looked good in.

"Hurry up, Liv. The sun waits for no man. Neither do the frozen drinks."

She fingered the lacy, barely there bikini and grinned before she snatched the skimpy material from the drawer and walked by him to the bathroom, catching a whiff of his sexy cologne as she passed. Her sex clenched in response, but that was okay. She'd have her revenge soon enough.

Tropical scents filled the air, and the sun beat down on the glorious white-sand beaches and swaying palm trees as they walked to the Kasbah pool. Although Dylan would like nothing more than to hit the Oasis (the adults-only pool) with Olivia, he wanted to make sure Nick Maddox and his family had settled in okay. He might have time to relax, but he was always on duty. He had a feeling Liv had forgotten that little fact when he'd rolled off her earlier.

Leaving her in that bed hadn't been easy, but if he'd given in to the desire to strip her naked, they'd never make it outside. Of course, she was repaying him now with that skimpy bathing suit she'd stridden out of the bathroom wearing. He wasn't even certain he could call it a bathing suit. More like a few pieces of string holding up tiny triangles that barely covered her gorgeous breasts, her sexy ass, or that pussy he was dying to taste again.

He placed a hand on the small of her back, his fingers gliding over the lace cover-up she'd chosen for their walk to the pool. Too bad he already knew what lay underneath.

He shifted as he walked, knowing he wasn't helping himself by thinking anything about Olivia right now. *Family pool*, he reminded himself. It didn't help douse the erection he was sporting.

"Look, there's some of the guys." Olivia pointed toward the bar, where Big held court.

"Hey, team! Join me!" Big waved them over to the bar, where he was, as promised, drinking a frozen margarita from a glass that, by most standards, would look huge. But since Big boasted such a strong, powerful frame, his hands dwarfed the glass.

Dylan shot Olivia a worried look.

"Don't worry. He can't get drunk on virgin froufrou drinks. It's all for show. Without his cousin around, he knows better than to get drunk and out of control. He told me as much himself," Olivia said.

Dylan let out a relieved breath until she muttered, "I hope," under her breath.

Flynn and Big were hanging with some beautiful women, and Dylan opted to wave and move on. "Do you want to sit under one of the umbrellas?" he asked.

"Sure." They headed for a free set of seats. "Don't you love the way the buildings and this whole area is structured like a Spanish-style resort? And the pool is lit up inside. I can imagine how gorgeous it looks at night!"

Her enthusiasm was contagious, and he reached, squeezing her hand.

She glanced up at him and smiled, and warmth pervaded his system. Yeah, there was something special about her or, at least, how he felt about her.

A cabana boy walked over and helped set up the chairs with towels, positioned the umbrella for Olivia's comfort, and offered them drinks. He settled into the chair and watched as Olivia, still standing, pulled her shirt off, exposing her bikini and that sexy body for view.

Drooling didn't begin to describe his reaction, but somehow he kept himself in check, even when she began to slowly cover herself with sunscreen, her delicate fingers rubbing the cream into her skin. She didn't glance at him, didn't acknowledge that he was watching, but his dick was hard, and he had the feeling she knew exactly the effect she had on him.

He blew out a breath, shoved his earbuds into his ears, and turned on the music app on his phone. Hard rock blared in his ears, distracting him—exactly what he needed.

As time passed, more people joined them around the pool, and soon Nick and his family arrived. They stopped by Dylan's chair, and he pulled the earbuds out.

"Hey, Nick. Glad you made it."

"Glad to be here." He glanced at Olivia. "Hi, Miss Dare."

"Olivia, please. Is this your wife?" Liv asked, sitting up in her seat and discreetly pulling her shirt over her exposed body.

Dylan held back a smirk, because now he knew she'd been deliberately flaunting her body to torture him. She was inherently shy, and obviously, when there were people around—especially team members—she didn't want them ogling her nearly nude body.

"Maria, this is Olivia Dare, the team's executive director, and Dylan Rhodes, our travel guy. He's the one who makes sure we stay in fantastic places like this one." Nick grinned at his wife, who held a well-covered baby in her arms.

"Nice to meet you, Maria. And everyone, please, call me Olivia."

"Hi, Olivia. Dylan," Maria, an attractive woman with her dark hair pulled into a high ponytail, said. "I hope I'll get to talk to you both later, but I want to get this little one into the cabana and out of the sun."

Olivia nodded. "I understand. I'm sure we'll find time later to talk."

"Come on, babe." Nick placed a hand on his wife's back and steered her toward the back of the pool and the extremely expensive covered cabanas. Nick, both in personality and ability, deserved the best the team could offer him.

"Want to take a swim?" Dylan asked her when the family was out of sight.

She blew out a breath and nodded. "That sounds great. It's brutally hot out here."

He rose and extended his hand, offering to help her up.

She shot him a grateful look and placed her palm in his. He helped her to her feet, unable to keep his eyes off her hot body. From the way she eyed his chest, the feeling was mutual. He shifted to the side, wishing he could discreetly adjust himself. He was rock hard and needed to get under the water immediately before everyone around the pool knew what he wanted to do to Olivia and damned whoever was watching.

They started in the shallow end, walking down the wide steps inside the pool. She had one hand on the metal bar and eased into the comfortable water. She hit the second step down and pushed off, gliding through the water and cooling off her body, the ends of her hair trailing through the water.

He caught up with her with one good push off the step ledge and grabbed her around the waist, backing her into the wall.

"Dylan!" she squealed in surprise, but she didn't look unhappy with his approach.

Knowing how important appearances were to her and aware of proper decorum himself, considering he was technically on the job, he glanced around. Sure enough, people were either sunbathing or too preoccupied reading, talking, or splashing one another to care what he and Olivia were up to.

She met his gaze and shyly snaked her arms around his neck. Two of the things he found most endearing about her were her honest reactions and lack of pretense. She wasn't bold and certain in dealing with him, and he respected that. He needed to be aware of her uncertainty and occasional insecurity, but he hoped that, in time, she'd lose those inhibitions.

"You feel good here, in my arms." He pulled her against him, and she wrapped her legs around his waist beneath the water.

"I like it here," she admitted.

He pressed a kiss to her damp lips. "Let's have dinner here tonight. They have a restaurant, and you can rent private cabanas where they'll serve you."

She raised an eyebrow. "Really? That sounds great!"

"Just you and me," he clarified.

Her smile widened.

Without warning, a splash of water hit them both, leaving them soaking wet.

"Kyle Andrew Lerner!" a woman called out angrily. "I told you, no splashing! Apologize to those people right now, and then out of the pool for a time-out."

Dylan glanced at the mother, who was fairly young herself. She had a toddler at the steps across the way, and she was pointing toward the empty pool chair right near her, where she obviously expected her son to sit.

Dylan's gaze shifted as a little boy, around eight, looked up at them with big brown eyes filled with tears, his bottom lip trembling. "Sorry," he said, then turned and made a beeline toward his mom.

"She's a good parent," Dylan murmured.

His own mother wouldn't have cared whether or not he splashed another person. She wouldn't have bothered with discipline unless he kept her from doing something *she* wanted to do. And most importantly, she wouldn't have taken him to a pool for fun, never mind on a vacation of any kind.

He drew a deep breath and refocused on Olivia. Her gaze was still on the little boy, who was now pulling himself out of the pool.

"I feel for the kid," Dylan said. "Gotta be embarrassing getting yelled at by your mom in front of strangers. And having to apologize. But she did well with him."

Olivia swallowed hard. "Yeah. She did." She pulled away from him and started for the far stairs nearest to their seats.

Dylan narrowed his gaze. "Liv, wait up!"

He followed her out of the pool, where she grabbed her towel off the seat and wrapped it around herself like protective armor.

"Hey, what just happened?" he asked.

She shook her head, her eyes damp. He needed to let it go, and he would. For now, but not for long. Obviously something about the episode had affected her deeply. Dylan's reaction to the boy went back to his childhood. Had Olivia's? Or was there something more?

He'd let her push him away, tell him she had issues, but if they wanted a relationship, something real, he needed answers. And she needed to decide whether or not he was worth the risk.

Chapter Six

*F*ollowing the afternoon at the pool, she and Dylan headed up to the room. She decided to lie down and take a short nap, while he opted to take a quick shower and go explore the resort and check on some things for later in the week.

Once he walked out, she opened her eyes. She hadn't been able to sleep, but she wasn't in the mood for either conversation or his curious looks. She'd had a freak reaction to the little boy at the pool, and now she felt ridiculous. Especially since she seemed to have these reactions around Dylan. Apparently, being with him evoked deep feelings and poked at old wounds.

She stared at the ceiling and replayed the incident. The splashing reminded her of her siblings. They'd never been able to behave on vacations their mom took them on, and really, there were too many of them for her to corral everyone into submission alone. Her dad had rarely joined them. In fact, she could barely remember a family vacation that had included him. But her mom had always been able to count on Ian.

As the oldest and the one with the biggest sense of responsibility, he'd always played the man of the house. From too young an age. Another thing that was her father's fault. But thanks to her mom, who loved them and made sure they had as normal a childhood as possible, and thanks to Ian, who did act like the father figure, they hadn't grown up like heathens, she thought, grinning.

But she quickly sobered when she remembered that moment in the pool when she'd glanced at the young mom with a toddler, now in her arms. Olivia's thoughts had turned to herself and her baby. The one she'd lost.

She pulled herself out of the bed, grabbed a sundress, a bra, and panties, and headed for the shower. Though she'd brought her toiletries from home, she liked the fresh scent of the shampoo and conditioner this luxury hotel provided. She lathered up with the matching body wash and rinsed off the sunscreen from today.

She wished her thoughts were on Dylan and how his erection had pulsed against her sex while underneath the water earlier, but instead, she was focused on how she kept pushing him away. He'd wanted to know what was bothering her when she'd fled the pool, and she knew it was time to tell him. She couldn't keep giving him half stories and asking him to wait. But she also didn't know if she had the nerve to dig into that time of her life.

After shaving her legs, lathering up with the shampoo, and using the thick conditioner on her hair, she rinsed and stepped from the shower. Next time something came up between them or the time was right, she wouldn't run. She'd talk. She didn't doubt he'd listen or understand. That wasn't her fear.

She feared that after she unloaded all her deepest pain, nothing would change inside her. That she'd still be afraid to move forward. Alone or with Dylan.

Dylan didn't return to the room until much later. She hadn't asked where he'd been, respecting his need for privacy. If they hadn't been forced to share a room, she wouldn't know what he did with his time until they met up for dinner. She read a book on the terrace and enjoyed the beauty of the mountain view.

After he returned, he pulled clothing out of the drawers and closet and changed for dinner while she put finishing touches on her makeup.

A few minutes later, he walked out of the changing area, looking handsome in a pair of khaki pants and a pale-blue T-shirt. "Ready for dinner?"

She strode over and placed her hands on his waist, determined to bridge the distance she kept inadvertently putting between them. "I am."

He tipped his head and brushed his lips over hers. "Good. Because you're going to love this setup."

"I can't wait."

He clasped her hand, and they headed out of the room. This time, he directed them toward the Oasis pool, an adults-only area. Beneath the darkening sky, the sun had begun to set, lighting the mountain with an orange glow.

They approached the pool area, where tents with white tops and gauzy curtains gave each person complete privacy, even more, she assumed, when darkness set in. A tingle of excitement and awareness trickled through her, knowing she and Dylan would be alone behind the sheathed walls.

He led her to a cabana in the far corner. No one seemed to be in the one next to them.

"This is it." He pushed back the curtain, and she stepped into an area dimly lit with lanterns. A long sofa gave them a place to sit in front of a low table set with an array of tapas and finger foods.

She stepped into their own private world and sighed at how intimate and perfect the setting was. "Dylan, you went all out."

"Only the best for you," he said in a husky voice. To her surprise, he pulled on a cord and released the sheeting that dropped down, covering the entry. "Complete privacy. I've instructed we not be disturbed."

They were alone in their own little world.

"Have a seat," he said with a sweep of his hand toward the lounger.

She lowered herself onto the sofa and crossed her legs beneath her.

He seated himself beside her, his leg touching hers.

"Hungry?" he asked.

Her stomach rippled with a combination of nerves and desire, but she was aware of the fact that she hadn't eaten dinner and somehow managed a nod.

"Good, because I'm starving." He infused the word with a double meaning she couldn't mistake. His fingers trailed a path along her spine, and she shivered, her nipples puckering beneath the soft material of her dress.

"This night is about you." He paused. "Us, really. I thought we could really get to know each other. Ask me anything and I'll answer. And I can do the same with you. Okay?"

Olivia trembled, but this time, it had nothing to do with sexual desire. Tonight was special. Meaningful. He'd gone to a lot of time and effort to set this up for her. Them. She didn't want to ruin it by blubbering about her past. But she did want to know about him, and he deserved to learn more about her. So if he asked a question that led to the baby conversation, she'd tell him. If not, she'd wait, because if anything was a mood killer, that would be. And despite the get-to-know-each-other game, the stage had been set for seduction. And she wanted that too.

He remained silent, waiting for an answer.

"Okay," she murmured.

He grinned. "And so we begin. Do you like sweet potatoes?" he asked, taking her off guard. From the grin on his face, he knew it too.

His question had the desired effect. She relaxed and laughed. "Yes, I love them."

He picked up what looked like an orange tater tot and held it in front of her. "Open."

She leaned forward and parted her lips. He popped the potato inside. She deliberately closed her mouth around his finger.

His gaze narrowed, and he drew in a shallow breath. She sucked on his salty digit briefly before letting go, and she chewed the delicious food, closing her eyes and moaning as she savored the explosion of sweet potato flavor.

"Do not make that sound unless you want me to act on it," he said gruffly.

She couldn't hold back a grin. "Sorry."

"No, you're not. Now . . . favorite color?" he asked, again surprising her. Was he building up to the more difficult, personal questions?

"Turquoise."

"I should have known it wouldn't be just blue."

She shrugged. "What's yours?" she asked, picking up a piece of pita bread and dipping it into hummus.

"Navy."

She smiled and held out the bread, allowing him to take a bite. He played nice and didn't touch her fingers with his mouth, but she squirmed, thinking of the possibility.

"Your turn to think up a question," he said when he finished chewing.

"Favorite holiday and why?" she asked.

"July Fourth. Love the fireworks."

He chose a generic holiday, not one associated with warm family feelings, making her feel bad.

She sampled a bite of a chicken wrap and was mortified when sauce ended up on her face. Before she could grab a napkin, he swiped the sauce with his finger and licked the remainder off, his gaze never leaving hers.

"Favorite holiday?" he asked without missing a beat.

That was easy. "Thanksgiving because no matter what my father did, my mom always made sure we had a traditional family dinner," she said honestly.

Shadows flickered behind his eyes, and she knew she'd been right. He didn't have fun family holidays to look back on.

They continued to eat and exchange tidbits of information. Favorite book, song, type of movie. They both liked action films, and he was glad she didn't pick sappy romantic comedies. By the time they finished eating or, rather, by the time they finished feeding each other, they had a solid knowledge of their likes and dislikes, and she realized they had a lot in common. They'd also have to compromise on sports during non-football season, as she wasn't a basketball fan and Dylan was.

"I'm full," she said, unable to eat another bite.

"One more question."

"I love dogs, not cats, but my building doesn't allow pets," she said, guessing at what had to be the only subject they hadn't covered.

"Have you ever been in love?" he asked, his expression schooled and unreadable.

She blinked in surprise. "Was that your plan? Ask the easy questions, lull me into a false sense of security, and then hit me hard?"

"I have to answer the same question," he reminded her.

She blew out a long breath. "I thought I was. But then I saw the type of person he really was, and I realized I couldn't possibly be in love with someone who could—cheat." She chickened out at the last minute, opting for the truth, just not all of it.

Dylan frowned at her answer. "Your boyfriend cheated on you?" he asked.

"I wouldn't have said it if it weren't true." She looked away, embarrassed.

"Hey. It's no reflection on you. It's his stupidity."

"Thank you." She met Dylan's dark gaze. "I have a different question for you to answer."

A muscle ticked in his jaw. "Go for it."

She grinned, seeing that he wasn't thrilled when the shoe was on the other foot. "Why did you and Meg break up?" She not only wanted to know—she needed to.

"Check and mate," he said, shaking his head.

"I don't play chess."

"But you did just corner me."

She grinned, pleased with herself. "Well?"

"When the time came to go away to school, I had to ask myself if it was worth the risk to break up and maybe lose her just so I could see other women." He paused, obviously giving the memory serious thought. "I decided it was . . . and that made me realize I didn't really love her. We were just used to each other."

She exhaled the breath she hadn't been aware of holding.

"Is that a smile I see?" he asked.

She shrugged. "You spend a lot of time talking to her. It's good to know how you really feel."

"Now are we finished talking about exes?"

"I should hope so."

"Good. Because I'd rather focus on how I feel about you." He leaned over, pressing her back into the cushions, his lower body in direct contact with hers.

"Feel that?" he asked of his hard, firm erection.

She opened her mouth to answer, but a needy moan came out instead. It was heady, knowing he'd gone to all this effort to make a special evening for them, that she could arouse him and make him want her as much as she wanted him.

"I like hearing what I do to you." He nuzzled his mouth behind her ear and sucked on her skin.

Ripples of awareness rocketed through her body, and she writhed beneath him, wanting more.

"You know we're alone here, right? Nobody will come in."

She shivered at the intent in his tone.

As he spoke, he pulled the strap of her dress over one shoulder and pressed soft kisses over her bared flesh. He continued to unveil her body, sliding her other strap down until her dress settled around her middle.

"Lift up."

She did as he asked, and he stood long enough to slide the material down her legs, letting it pool on the floor. He stood over her, desire in his gaze, and her stomach tumbled in the best possible way.

"Do you know what I'm going to do to you?"

"I hope you're going to make love to me."

His eyes darkened at her words. "Yes." The word came out on a hiss. "But first I'm going to taste every inch of you." He placed one knee on the edge of the sofa and straddled her hips.

"You're still dressed." She reached for his shirt and slid her hands beneath the soft tee. His abs were firm and warm, and she inched her fingers upward, scraping her nails over his nipples.

He shuddered, letting out a low groan.

"I want to feel your skin against mine," she murmured.

He lifted the shirt and pulled it roughly over his head, then his lips came down hard on hers. But that wasn't all. He fell on her, the defined planes of his chest pressing hard against hers. The scrape of his hair, the heat of his body, the ravenous way his mouth devoured hers all worked to make her feel wanted in a way she never had been before.

In a way she feared she never would be again.

Dylan's hunger for Olivia warred with his need to slow down, to treat her right, to take her slowly. To make her feel how special she was to him. But she scraped her nails against his chest—and his cock, already at attention, grew even harder. He ground his dick against the cradle of her hips, and she moaned loudly at the contact. Too loud, even though he'd ensured they didn't have neighbors.

Good thing he'd come prepared. He reached into his pocket and pulled out a silk scarf.

"What's that for?" she asked, eyes wide. And interested.

Fuck. "Much as I wouldn't mind getting kinky and tying you up, this is actually to make sure you don't bring security running in here with your loud moans."

Her lips parted in a cute *oh*. "Really?"

"Unless you think you can keep it quiet." He rocked his cock directly against her clit.

Her eyes rolled and she groaned.

"Thought not. Although I love hearing those screams, I'd rather keep this between us. You okay with that?"

Her eyes remained wide, but she nodded, her trust in him humbling. "We'll tie you up another time," he promised.

"I think I'd like that."

He winked at her and gently slid the silk between her lips. "Now you can groan, but it won't sound as loud. If it gets uncomfortable, just tap me on the shoulder, okay?"

She nodded.

"Lift your head." She did, and he tied the knot behind her head, careful not to pull too tight. He kissed her lips lightly and continued his work before she panicked at being gagged. He unhooked her lace bra with the front clasp, slid the straps over her arms, and piled it on top of her dress. He left her scrap of panties on. For now.

He glanced down. She was spread out before him, arms at her sides, legs parted in invitation. Her panties were damp, wet with her desire. And her small but sexy breasts tipped up, nipples puckered, demanding attention he was all too happy to give.

She was fucking gorgeous. He bent his head and licked around one nipple, deliberately teasing her, testing her responsiveness. She arched her back, a clear signal she wanted more. He grinned and nibbled on her breast before sliding his tongue across her chest to the other side, providing the same tormenting treatment to her other tight bud.

She moaned, and her body thrashed beneath his. He continued to lave her soft skin, inhaling her unique scent, and though he hadn't thought he could get any harder, he did. He continued licking around her areola, enjoying the needy sounds escaping her throat.

He glanced up, met her gaze, and caught the flash of heat in her eyes. He licked lightly over one nipple. Her gaze narrowed, and she whimpered.

"Need more, sunshine?"

She nodded, and he bit down lightly on her nipple. Her hips shot upward, her sex grinding against his aching erection.

"I love how sensitive you are."

He alternated nibbles and licks, loving laps of his tongue with harsher deliberate flickers that had her nipples hard as rocks. He played her body, and she responded beautifully, keeping it going until her whimpers were overlapping, her hips rolling beneath his.

He slid down on her legs, taking her thin strip of panties along with him. He braced his hands on her thighs, parted her legs, and dipped his head so he could really begin his feast for the night.

He couldn't remember the last time he'd enjoyed going down on a woman so damned much. When her responses had meant everything. He liked giving a woman pleasure— only a dickhead wouldn't. But this was something else. The musky scent that was Olivia's alone, the pale thighs around his head, and the slick pink pussy waiting for him. He took in every last sensation before sliding his tongue over her for a thorough lick.

"Mmmm." Her back arched, and he nuzzled her sex with his nose before playing her with his tongue. He licked up and down her outer lips, bit lightly on each, and had her squeezing him tightly between her thighs.

He eased one finger inside her, and her slick heat closed around him. He groaned into her, and the vibrations had her trembling around him. He added a second finger and lifted his head. "Okay, babe?"

She nodded, eyes wild, her entire body slick with sweat and trembling.

Yeah, this was what he wanted. Her completely at his mercy. "Think you can handle another?" he asked.

Because he wanted to fill her and make her come this way first, before taking her with his cock, slamming into her over and over like a wild man. Because he couldn't imagine this ending any other way. So he wanted to make sure he gave her all he could first.

She nodded, and he added another finger inside her. Her low moan shook him hard, and he began pumping in and out, adding hard flicks of his tongue over her taut clit. Back and forth, he played with the tiny bud until she screamed as best she could with the scarf muffling her cries. He flattened his tongue against her sex while curling his fingers inside her. Her entire body drew tight, and she stiffened for a moment before riding out her climax, her sex grinding against his tongue and mouth, her inner walls clenching around his fingers.

He looked up to see her cheeks flushed, eyes closed, the most intense, blissful expression on her beautiful face. He slowed his movements as she came down from her climax and paused to rest against her thigh.

He pressed a long kiss against her hot flesh before easing himself up beside her. Her eyes were still closed.

He gently lifted her head and undid the loose knot, pulling the silk off her mouth. "You okay?" he asked.

"Never better," she murmured, a satisfied, loopy smile on her face that *he'd* put there. "You've got talent," she murmured, still obviously dazed.

He grinned. "What can I say? You inspire me to do my best."

Her eyes warmed at his comment. "Dylan?"

"Yeah?"

"I still feel empty," she admitted, meeting his gaze.

Thank God, because he thought his cock was going to explode. "You're up for more?"

She arched her hips toward him in reply.

Okay then. He quickly undid his pants and slid them off, along with his boxer briefs. But not before retrieving a condom from a pocket and placing it on the couch beside him.

"You're like a Boy Scout today. So prepared."

He laughed. "Yeah, well, no Boy Scout should be doing what I am."

She rolled her eyes at that. "Come here." She held out her arms.

He knew Olivia, knew how she guarded herself—her body and her heart. Their first time in her apartment had been a long time coming and explosive because of it. She took small steps with him, and mentions of her past sent her running. But she was trying now, and he understood that this gesture had meaning.

He joined their hands together, lifting her arms over her head. "I'm really glad you're here now." He kissed her nose. "With me. Like this."

She sighed. "I can't resist you when you're sweet."

"I can't resist you at all." He kissed her hard on the lips before releasing her hands and picking up the condom.

"Let me," she said in a husky voice.

He blinked in surprise and handed her the packet. She opened it with little finesse and shaking hands. With no expertise behind her actions, she reached for his painfully hard erection and slid the rubber down his shaft. Her hand lingered too long at the base, her fingers cupping his balls.

"Enough," he said roughly. "If you touch me again, I'm going to embarrass myself," he said, needing to explain.

"I like that I can get you as hot as you get me." She grasped his cock once more.

He groaned and took control, bracing his hands on either side of her, poised for entry, her hand still gripping him, harder now.

He slid the head over her clit, and she moaned loudly. He didn't stop her this time.

"I can't wait," he said, teeth clenched.

"Then don't."

He pushed himself inside her, finding her hot and wet for him. Once assured she was ready, he thrust all the way home and stilled. "You feel so fucking good."

He glided out, her hot pussy gripping him every step of the way. "Bend your knees."

She did as he asked, and that gave him more room to move, allowed him to press deeper with each successive thrust.

"Oh God." She whimpered and met him thrust for thrust. "Harder. I need you to fuck me harder."

He loved when she let go of her inhibitions and fears, when she was just his. He had no problem giving her what she needed.

They sought their climax together; every slam of his hips was accompanied by her increasingly loud but muffled cries. He lost track of time and place, his entire being focused on the woman writhing beneath him. She sucked him into her body and cushioned him in heat until his orgasm loomed large. His spine tingled, his balls drew up tight, almost painfully as he thrust deep, and she shattered.

"Dylan!" She arched into him, and he managed to hold off his own climax while she rode out her own. Her sex ground against him until she took him along with her for the ride.

Chapter Seven

Olivia woke up in the big bed in the suite she shared with Dylan. She recalled their evening and how he'd carried her back to the room, ignoring the catcalls and whistles of people as they'd walked. Honestly, she'd been so exhausted she hadn't cared.

She rolled onto her back to find his dark eyes watching her.

"Everything good?" he asked.

She didn't blame him. She had a tendency to pull away, but she had no intention of doing so this morning. "I'm good." She crawled closer. "Very, very good."

She was sore in the best possible ways; a gorgeous man had gone out of his way to make her night special and to make sure she'd come quite a few times . . . Yeah, she was more than good!

He smiled in obvious relief.

"So what's on today's agenda?" she asked.

"We have the day free. Breakfast?"

She nodded. They ended up sharing a shower, which delayed getting to breakfast, because Dylan's definition of getting clean involved a whole lot of getting dirty first. With the hot water streaming over them and her arms braced against the wall, he still managed to snag a condom and to take her from behind, filling her up and giving her another experience she'd never forget.

By the time they walked through the lobby for breakfast, it was almost ten thirty a.m. On the way to the restaurant, she caught sight of Big sprinting across the open area toward the front door.

"Marcus!" Dylan called out.

The other man stopped at the sound of his name. He turned and caught Olivia's gaze, immediately looking away.

They strode up to him together.

"Where's the fire?" Dylan asked him.

"Huh?"

Olivia bit her lip. "No, umm, what's your rush?" she tried to explain. "Where are you off to?"

He glanced around nervously. "I'm just, uh, taking a walk."

Dylan narrowed his gaze. "You don't lie well, Marcus. What gives?"

"You'll be mad, and I'll get in trouble." For all his size and weight, Marcus was still very much a kid, probably less mature than the average twenty-four-year-old. Of course, the average twenty-four-year-old didn't get tossed into heartthrob million-aire status right out of college.

Olivia exchanged a worried glance with Dylan. "Is your cousin here?" she asked.

"No!" he said too quickly, still not meeting her gaze.

"Okay, well, then go," Dylan said. "And take care."

Marcus darted for the revolving door, and Olivia turned to Dylan. "What was that all about? Why did you let him go?"

"Because he's an adult who deserves the chance to make the right choices. We can't babysit him. We just have to hope for the best."

"In theory, I agree. In reality, Ian sent me to keep an eye on him too."

Dylan grasped her hand. "There's keeping an eye on him, and there's babysitting. You can't just follow him around twenty-four seven."

She sighed. "I hate it when you're right."

"Don't you know by now? I'm *always* right."

She elbowed him in the side. "And I'm always starving. Let's go before I'm forced to comment on that statement."

They turned and headed for the restaurant once more, but Olivia couldn't stop thinking about Marcus . . . and she had a gut feeling trouble would definitely be coming. She only hoped any fallout didn't hit her, as well as Marcus.

To her pleasant surprise, trouble didn't follow Marcus that day or the next. They attended all the Pro Bowl–related parties and press events. And when they weren't talking business, she and Dylan spent time alone, their relationship growing. It was a novel experience, allowing herself to enjoy without worry—but he made it easy. And without the real world to intrude, she actually relaxed.

The morning of the Pro Bowl, the players had interviews scheduled at the tailgate party in the VIP tent. The sun shone, and the day was warm, perfect for the musical celebrity talent to play outside. Dylan and Olivia showed up early, making sure the players were comfortable and had what they needed. Olivia was having a blast. The casual atmosphere allowed her to wear a comfortable sleeveless dress, and she pulled her hair up in a sleek ponytail to help her avoid getting sweaty and hot.

Players from every team mingled, some accompanied by their families, all with smiles on their faces. All but Marcus, who was nowhere to be found.

"Where is he?" Dylan asked, teeth clenched, his annoyance palpable. The time for the man's interview in the broadcast booth was inching closer. "We should have met him in the lobby and traveled to the stadium together."

"He isn't a child, as you pointed out. We didn't think we needed to make sure he met his limo at the hotel this morning."

Dylan frowned, and she couldn't help but smooth the wrinkles in his forehead with her finger. He groaned at the intimate touch.

"Not the time," he muttered, but his voice dropped to that husky tone that got her insides revving.

Of course, just looking at Dylan in his dark pants and white shirt with aviators on his eyes, and it didn't matter that she'd had him inside her earlier this morning. She wanted him again, as evidenced by the pulsing between her thighs.

She swallowed a groan of her own. "Don't worry. I'll do my best to track him down," she said, focusing on what was important.

"Are you sure you don't mind?"

"You stay and keep an eye on the others," she assured him.

She walked away from the tailgate, stopping when she knew she could hear better on her phone. She hoped there wasn't anything seriously wrong and that Marcus had just overslept.

First, she called the hotel and asked for his room. No answer. She called back and asked the operator if either she or Dylan had had any messages left for them, hoping maybe Marcus had tried to get in touch.

"I'm sorry. There's nothing," the woman who'd answered the phone said.

"Can you connect me with the concierge?" she asked. When a man answered, she asked if anyone had seen Marcus get into his scheduled limousine that morning.

"Actually, I did see him."

"Are you sure it was him?"

"Positive. Because another man met up with him at the car. Yelled out his name."

Olivia narrowed her gaze. "Did you see what the other man looked like?" she asked.

"Sorry. They argued a bit and then climbed into the car. I was busy and didn't get a look at him," the concierge said.

"How long ago?"

"About forty minutes?"

"Thank you." Late but on his way.

Olivia pulled out her cell and was about to check in with Dylan when she caught sight of Marcus just inside the tent.

She rushed to catch up with him, pushing through the crowd. Thanks to his size, she was able to spot him easily and called out, "Marcus!"

He turned toward her, and her stomach plummeted. His white dress shirt was rumpled and half-untucked, and there was no tie to be found. Worse, his eyes were red and glassy, and he didn't look anywhere near ready to talk to reporters, let alone play football.

She strode up to him and clasped his arm. "Marcus!"

"Miss Olivia!" He stepped toward her, but his gait was unsteady.

"Where have you been?" she asked in a low voice.

"Trying to be good. I really was. But—"

"Can I get your autograph?" a young boy asked.

"Sure." Marcus grinned at the kid. Olivia waited for him to sign his name on the boy's piece of paper, then grabbed his massive arm and pulled him away from people.

"Where are we going?" he asked, genuinely confused.

"To talk where we can't be overheard or interrupted. Come on. Over here." She led him to an empty picnic table. "Have you been drinking?"

"No, but I'm not feeling well. I think I have a virus or something. I'm dizzy."

She blew out a breath. "Can you play today?"

He shrugged. "Not sure." The big football player turned blue eyes on her. "Wendell said it would pass, but I think I'm getting worse."

"Wendell?" Olivia asked, her voice rising.

The other man cringed. "Well, yeah. He's here in Arizona," he said, dropping his head. "That day you saw me, Wendell called and asked me to meet him. I did it, only to tell him he couldn't stay."

Olivia blew out a breath. "What happened?"

"He said he understood. We talked and he left." Marcus ran a hand through his blond hair. "Then he showed up at my room this morning. Said he wanted to wish me luck before the game. Said he wasn't going to cause trouble. He just wanted to have breakfast with me and he'd go. He's my cousin. I couldn't say no." His worried, glassy eyes begged her to believe.

Olivia nodded. "So what happened? Are you sure you didn't drink with him?"

"We ate. I had bacon and eggs, and I just drank orange juice, I swear. But my stomach started to bother me soon after. So Wendell rode here in the limo with me in case I didn't feel well."

So Wendell was *here* at the event. That was trouble nobody needed, and Olivia's stomach plummeted. At least he couldn't get inside the event without a press pass or ticket, and the Thunder hadn't issued him one of those.

Still, a sudden wave of apprehension washed over her. "Where is Wendell now?" she asked.

Marcus mumbled the answer.

"What did you say?"

"You're going to be mad at me."

"Just tell me." She clenched her fists, already knowing the answer.

"I gave him my extra guest pass."

"Okay, we need to get you examined by a doctor, and then if you can't play, it will be done officially."

She texted Dylan. *Found him. Problem. He's sick.*

Her phone buzzed, and she scanned Dylan's reply. *On my way.*

She texted back. *Meet at entrance to pavilions.*

"Come on." She stood and pulled on Marcus's arm.

He sluggishly walked with her to the entrance to the tent. "Are you okay?" she asked him.

"I'm nauseous and—"

"There you are!" Wendell called out.

Olivia glanced in the direction of the other man's voice. Unlike his cousin, Wendell wasn't dressed for a VIP event. He wore cutoff jean shorts and an ill-fitting football jersey, too big on his lean frame. He wasn't good-looking like Marcus, nor was he mild-mannered. Even if Marcus's clothes were disheveled, he knew he was supposed to be properly attired. He represented the team. Wendell represented Marcus and, by extension, the Thunder.

One look at Wendell, and Olivia could see the leashed anger beneath the surface. She'd thought it the first time they'd met at a Thunder practice he'd attended, and she noticed it again now.

"I've been looking everywhere for you, cuz." Wendell slapped Marcus on the back.

Marcus shook his head at the sight of the other man. "You promised to walk around, check things out, and go." He glanced at Olivia. "He swore this was the last time he'd be around. He's going home tomorrow, aren't you, Wendell?"

The mean gleam in the other man's eyes said otherwise.

"Where are you two off to?" Wendell asked, ignoring the question.

Olivia stepped up to answer. "I'm taking him to see a doctor. And you need to get out of here too."

Wendell's eyes narrowed. "Who do you think you are, telling me to leave?" he asked in a loud voice.

Olivia winced as people around them turned to look.

"Marcus is my family. You have no right to tell me what to do!" Wendell continued ranting.

"Come on, man. Don't do this here." Marcus put a hand on his cousin's shoulder.

Wendell shrugged it off, pushing at Marcus so the drugged player stumbled. He caught himself and stood up straighter, staring at his relative, surprise and hurt in his gaze.

Poor Marcus, Olivia thought. He was too naïve to be in this world, let alone deal one-on-one with a man like Wendell.

"Hey." Dylan walked over, stepping between the two men. "What's going on?"

"That bitch thinks she can tell me what to do." Wendell pointed a finger at Olivia.

"As the executive director of the team, she can," Dylan informed him.

"I'm not one of her players, and my cousin wants me here." Wendell glanced at Marcus for support, but he stood back, clearly ill and uncomfortable and not ready to pick sides.

Olivia straightened her shoulders. She intended to protect her player and the team's reputation. "You'd better think about your actions. Your cousin has a morals clause in his contract. The NFL has strict behavioral policies and expectations. And instead of you helping him follow those rules, you keep putting him in situations that violate them. The team has every right to ban you from events."

"Fuck that," Wendell said, his anger showing. "It's a free country. I can stay if I want to. And it's my job to take care of him." He pointed to Olivia. "And no bitch is going to tell me I can't," he said, his voice rising.

"That's enough." Dylan grasped Wendell's shoulder and turned him toward the parking lot. "You will not speak to her that way. You will not show up at team events. And you will stay the hell away from your cousin as long as he's under contract with the Thunder." Dylan grasped the man hard enough to give him a shake as he spoke.

"Take your hands off me!" Wendell tried to shrug free.

"Is everything okay here?" a security guard strode up to them and asked.

"This man shouldn't have been given a pass," Olivia said. "He needs to be escorted off the property."

The guard glanced at Olivia's name tag and then Dylan's. With an understanding nod, he took hold of Marcus's cousin and walked the belligerent man out to the parking lot. He fought and argued the entire way.

"Ms. Olivia, Mr. Rhodes, I'm sorry. I—"

Dylan held up a hand to cut Marcus off.

"We need to get him to a doctor," Olivia said before Dylan could speak. "He's sick."

As if on cue, Marcus moaned and grabbed his stomach.

"I'll take him to medical. You stay and do what you need to for the other players. I'll text you, and we can meet up here or back at the hotel, depending on where I end up."

"Are you sure?" Olivia asked.

Dylan nodded. He leaned over and brushed his lips over Olivia's, and she took strength in that simple touch. She'd been able to handle Wendell, but her insides were still trembling. There was something about the man that wasn't just mean but dangerous. She couldn't be sure, but she suspected he'd put something in Marcus's food that had made him so sick, he couldn't play.

In any case, she hoped Marcus was right this time and Wendell would head on home. Unfortunately, she sensed they hadn't seen the last of Marcus Bigsby's cousin.

By the time someone on the medical staff checked Marcus out, he was burning up with fever. He wouldn't be playing in the Pro Bowl. So Dylan took Marcus back to the hotel in a cab and led the man directly up to his room. Marcus was full of apologies for Wendell's arrival in Arizona and for his own inability to play. He was visibly upset, but as soon as he lay down on the bed, he fell asleep.

Dylan sat in the outer room of Marcus's suite and began the process of damage control. The fact that Marcus wasn't playing would be big news, and Ian needed to get the PR team on things as soon as possible. He'd already informed Ian, who'd taken charge from Miami. He hired a private security guard to sit in the outer room and make sure Marcus didn't slip out . . . or Wendell slip in.

By the time the guard arrived to switch places with Dylan, the Pro Bowl was nearly over. Dylan had caught most of it on TV, and the sympathy factor was playing in Marcus's favor. *Crisis averted*, he thought as he headed down to his suite to wait for Olivia.

He must've fallen asleep, because he woke to find her curling against him on the bed, her hair damp, smelling fresh and fragrant from a shower.

His cock sprang to attention, as it always did when she was around. "I didn't hear you come in."

"That's because you were out cold."

He nodded. "How did the rest of the day go?" he asked.

"Fine." She shrugged. "Normal. How's Marcus?"

Dylan and Olivia already spoke on the phone, and she knew her brother had hired someone to watch over their sick star player.

"Still asleep as far as I know." He reached over and checked his phone. "No texts from his babysitter," Dylan muttered.

"Good." Olivia laid her head on his shoulder and groaned. "What a day."

"You can say that again."

"What a day," she muttered.

"Wise ass." He chuckled. "But on a more serious note, are you okay after that confrontation with Wendell?"

"He scared me," she admitted.

He pulled her close, but the thick terry cloth robe didn't allow him the access to her skin that he craved. Had been craving since the minute he'd seen the man bullying her.

All his protective instincts had gone into high gear, and he'd wanted nothing more than to smash the man's smug face. But he'd been aware of their location, and he knew better than to react with violence in front of an audience. But if the man ever touched her, he wouldn't make any promises.

"But you showed up, and everything's fine. And I really don't want to think about him now."

"Then what is it you want to do?" he asked in a gruff voice he barely recognized.

She reached her hand down and slid her fingers into his pants, wrapping her hand around his stiff cock. "I think that should be obvious," she said in a teasing tone, then pumped her hand up and down for good measure.

Olivia was wet. Not from the shower, but from wanting Dylan. She cupped his thick, hard erection in her palm. When a drop of precum slickened her fingertips, she curled her fingers tighter around him.

He grasped her wrist and stilled her hand. "You don't want to end this party before it gets started, do you?"

She shook her head. No, but she wanted him to take over. To do all sorts of naughty things to her while she lay at his mercy and just took what he gave her.

"Dylan?"

"What?" He pulled her on top of him, and though he was fully dressed and she was in a hotel robe, she felt his heat.

Knowing there was only one way to get what she wanted, she gathered her courage. "Remember the other night in the cabana? You brought the scarf?"

His gorgeous eyes darkened. "Yes."

"I want—" She hesitated, unsure of how to ask.

"Tell me," he said in a gruff voice. "Just say it and it's yours."

She slid her tongue over her lips. "I want you to tie me up," she whispered.

"God, you are so fucking perfect." He rolled her to the side of the bed, then rose and headed for the closet.

Her breath caught as she waited, her entire body primed for whatever would come next. She knew from slips that Riley made that her brother, Ian, liked to dominate in the bedroom, but she didn't know the details, thank goodness. And her cousins in New York had their kinky side. Their significant others had mentioned it as well. So when Dylan had pulled out a scarf the other night, she'd been . . . intrigued.

And definitely interested.

She quickly stripped off the robe and lay back on the bed to wait. He returned from the closet, tie in hand and wearing absolutely nothing. Her mouth watered at the delectable sight of his gorgeous body. Lean yet muscular, tanned, and just plain delicious. Her gaze swept from his cock, which stood proudly, to the silk material in his hand.

"Something tells me this is going to look better on you than it ever did on me." He paused as he stared at her with hunger in his eyes. "Up." He gestured toward the head of the bed.

She slid back against the pillows, unable to take her gaze from those hands and the way he wrapped the tie around his palms and stretched the material taut. Her sex grew slick with wet heat.

"You're gorgeous, baby. And I wish I could tie you to the headboard, but there're no slats on this thing." He studied her intently. "Hands in front of you."

She placed her palms together, and he came over, wrapping the soft tie around her wrists a few times and knotting it. *Rather easily*, she thought.

"How do you know what you're doing?" she asked.

"Friends. I went to a couple of clubs after I graduated high school."

She tilted her head to the side, curious. "Did you like it?"

He shrugged in answer. "Not a lifestyle for me, but it's fun. Good when both people are in the mood." He leaned back and studied his handiwork. Then he slid one finger over her pussy, through her sex, and dipped into her. "And you definitely are in the mood."

She threw her head back and shuddered, closing her eyes as she tried to clench tight and hold him inside.

He chuckled and pulled out, leaving her empty.

"Tease." She met his gaze and knew she was pouting, but she couldn't help it.

"I'm trying." He grinned and licked his finger, slick with her juices.

That was hot.

"Now. Let's get to the good stuff," he said.

"I'm waiting." She parted her legs in invitation, exposing her freshly shaved sex to him completely. Her solo shower had served multiple purposes—unwinding alone and getting ready for him.

"I really want to devour you," he said as he stared, his expression that of a man completely mesmerized. "But I don't think I can hold out long enough to get inside you if I do."

Either act would work for her, but his thick erection would satisfy her most, and she squirmed against the bed at the decadent thought. Her thighs clenched together but didn't provide enough friction or alleviate the growing, aching pressure. An embarrassing whimper escaped from her throat.

He leaned close and brushed her hair off her cheek. His musky scent enveloped her, and she couldn't wait until he pounded into her and she could bury her face in his neck and just inhale him while she came. "Oh God."

He pressed a gentle kiss to her lips. "You're okay, right?"

How he could be sweet and dominating at the same time was beyond her, but she loved it.

"I'm good." Beyond good, really. She was so aroused that she knew she'd come at the slightest touch.

She wanted to think about nothing but Dylan and the pleasure he could give.

"Hands and knees," he said, startling her.

She blinked. "I thought . . ."

He raised an eyebrow. "What? That you'd put your arms over your head and I'd fuck you missionary style?"

His question didn't really need an answer. That was exactly what she'd thought, and they both knew it.

"Well, I'd rather you feel me *everywhere*," he said, his voice hitting a deep octave. He patted the bed. "Hands. And. Knees."

Her breath hitched, and though she was nervous, she repositioned herself as he demanded. With her bound hands in front of her, she rose to her knees, her forearms and elbows taking most of her weight.

He placed a pillow beneath her stomach, raising her lower body a bit more. Silence followed, and she imagined him behind her, studying her, and stifled an embarrassed sound.

"You are fucking gorgeous."

She blushed and dipped her head, not knowing which part of her he was referring to.

He slid his palms over the globes of her ass, down her thighs, and back up again before cupping her sex in his big, warm hand. She moaned and arched her back, her pussy clenching and unclenching in needy pulses that wouldn't be denied.

The sound of foil ripping was an aphrodisiac to her already sensitized body, and she laid her cheek against the mattress, trying to catch her breath.

"Ready?" he asked.

"Mmm-hmm." She lifted her head and braced herself.

His arm wrapped around her waist as his cock pressed into her slick opening. He entered her slowly, her wet body accepting him easily, inch by gradual inch. It wasn't enough, and she arched back at the same moment he thrust forward, locking their bodies together deeper than ever before.

"Oh God." She groaned and dropped her head onto her hands.

"You can say that again." His big hand slid up her stomach until he cupped one breast against his palm. "Perfect fit," he muttered before he began teasing her nipple, playing, plucking, and rolling it between his fingers until she was writhing around his thick cock.

"Feel good?" he asked, still lodged deep.

"It'd be better if you'd move. I can't take it." She clenched her inner walls around him, hoping to entice him to fuck her hard.

"You can." His finger tweaked her nipple once more, and she shuddered, pushing back against him.

She'd expected him to pound into her. Instead, he rocked gently, hips swaying back and forth, the rhythm forcing his cock against that sensitive spot inside her. The one no man but him had ever reached.

Small ripples that felt suspiciously like the beginning of an orgasm swelled inside her. But he wasn't gliding in and out, wasn't doing anything except cradling her against his big body, rolling his hips against hers. And despite the fact that they weren't face-to-face, it was gentle and intense—seriously emotional—and a lump formed in her throat.

His hips rocked against her ass, and he was right. She felt him everywhere. She swallowed a sob, not understanding the emotions overtaking her. She didn't know she was so sensitive, so—"Close. Oh God, I'm close."

She felt her juices sliding between them, coating him, and suddenly his hand dropped lower, the pad of one finger pressing against her sex. "Come on, sunshine. Come for me just like this."

He ground his cock deep, and she cried out, the orgasm that hit her more explosive than any before, because he wasn't fucking her, he was loving her, and she'd be a fool to deny the obvious. Not when there was so much emotion washing over her.

She might still have been midorgasm when he pulled out, tossed the pillow, and rolled her onto her back. She raised her arms over her head and out of the way just as he thrust back into her with a tortured groan.

"Livvy, fuck." He jerked inside her once, twice, and she buried her face in his neck and inhaled him while she came, and he followed her over.

Chapter Eight

ylan awoke to an empty bed. Olivia had showered and was packing her suitcase when he dragged his ass out of bed. She shot him a smile, one he returned, but neither of them spoke.

He didn't know what to say. Last night had been intense. Serious emotional shit had passed between them, and he needed time to process. If her silence during the rest of the morning and trip to the airport was any indication, she felt the same way.

He'd told himself he was all in with her, ready for anything. But apparently, it was one thing to be so head over heels for a woman he couldn't think straight about and another to deal with the emotions the kind of sex they'd shared brought up.

She slept most of the flight back home, her head on a pillow against the window. Not on his shoulder. He swiped a hand over his eyes and leaned back against the uncomfortable seat.

He'd never, ever felt so much, and it scared the shit out of him. Not because he wasn't sure of his feelings but because he was.

He'd fallen in love with a woman who hadn't dealt with her past. If there was one thing he knew, old ghosts always showed themselves eventually. And he didn't want to be a casualty when Olivia's returned.

The week after Arizona flew by. As usual, while she'd been away, work had piled up. Olivia didn't mind. She thrived on doing her job. Dylan had to travel out of town midweek for an unexpected meeting with the hotel chain the team did business with. With him on the West Coast, where the main offices were located, and Olivia on the East Coast, they managed a few short phone calls in between his meetings.

Their last time together had been . . . intense, scary for a woman who rarely let herself get involved so deeply. She'd pulled back a bit, just needing time, and then he'd left on his trip. After twenty-four-seven time with Dylan, this break gave her more time than she'd wanted or needed away from him. She missed him like crazy and couldn't wait until he came home. He wasn't sure of his timing yet.

Friday night, she was so exhausted that she crawled into bed and fell asleep soon after her head hit the pillow. Too soon afterward, crazy knocking sounded from outside the bedroom door.

Olivia pulled the pillow over her head and groaned, but the noise didn't let up. "Go away!"

"No."

A peek revealed Avery—who else?—walking into the room. She jumped into the bed beside Olivia, the way she'd always done on the weekends when they were kids.

Olivia managed a tired smile for her sister.

"Why are you still in bed? You never sleep in."

"Let's see, there was a time difference in Arizona, and I've worked nonstop this whole week to catch up. I'm tired." Beyond tired. Even now, she couldn't stifle a yawn.

"Well, now you're up! And it's a good thing too, because the day doesn't wait for anyone." Avery jumped up and opened the blinds, letting the sun stream into the previously darkened room.

Olivia blinked into the glare, her eyes watering. "Are you crazy?"

"Nope. You need to get up. Dylan called me earlier. He couldn't reach you. He took a red-eye home. Anyway, he's going to be here any minute, and you need to get ready."

"He's home?" She couldn't hide the excitement in her voice, and her sister grinned.

Avery headed to the closet and began sorting through Olivia's dresses. "He said to tell you his sister is having a family barbecue for his niece's birthday, and he wants to bring you with him." Avery pulled out a halter dress with small pink flowers. "I think this dress will look pretty for an outdoor party, don't you?"

Olivia could pick out her own clothes, as they both knew, but Avery was a fashionista of the first order, and Olivia indulged her.

Still, she couldn't resist teasing her. "You do know I hate you this early in the morning, right? You're too perky, and I haven't had my coffee yet."

"You love me *and* my perkiness. So how do you feel about meeting his family?" Avery turned worried eyes her way.

Olivia's stomach did a little flip. She didn't know what would come of her relationship with Dylan, but he'd mentioned that his older sister was his family and that they were close. She really wanted to make a good impression. And wasn't that telling when it came to her feelings for the man?

She swallowed hard. "It's a first for me," she murmured.

"And that's why I'm here to help."

Olivia slid out of bed, glanced in the mirror, and cringed. "I need to shower."

"Then get moving! I told him you'd be up and ready."

"Neither one of you thought I might have other plans?" she asked.

Her sister grinned. "Not really. And even if you did, I knew you'd cancel them for this."

"Why does this feel like a setup?" Olivia muttered.

"Because I want you to be happy. And Dylan seems to do that for you. So when he called, I said you'd go with him. He'll be here soon, so move it."

"How can I be annoyed with you when you say nice things like that?"

"You can't."

With a sigh, Olivia pulled out sexy underwear from her drawer, in case she and Dylan ended up alone later, then picked up the dress Avery liked. A little while later, Olivia had managed to wake up, courtesy of Avery's coffee, a warm shower, and thoughts of seeing Dylan.

She was dressed and ready to see him. It was the first time they'd be alone since their time in Phoenix, and meeting his family, no less. She placed a hand over her nervous stomach. She didn't want to question too hard what it all meant—him bringing her with him and her serious nerves about meeting the people he loved.

She drew a deep breath and walked out of her bedroom, surprised to find Dylan drinking coffee with her sister. "Well, hi," she said. "I didn't hear the doorbell."

"He knocked," Avery said from where she sat at the table, feet propped on a chair.

Dylan rose to his feet. "Good morning." His voice slid over her like warm honey. Sweet and oh so good.

"Morning." She held out her empty coffee cup. "Is there any more for me?"

"You can get more on the road. We need to make a stop to buy toys on the way to my sister's."

She raised an eyebrow. "Toy shopping? Is that your new idea of a date?" she asked, teasing.

"Depends on what kind of toys we're looking for." His eyes darkened with a sensual look she recognized.

A look that had her pulse pounding and her body responding, ready for anything he desired.

"Just eew!" Avery said, jumping up from her seat. "Good thing I know this is just a Toys "R" Us trip. Go. Both of you." With a shake of her head, she headed for her room, closing the door behind her.

Olivia laughed, and Dylan merely grinned.

A few minutes later, she'd grabbed her purse, and they walked out the door.

"Well, this is a surprise," Olivia said as they waited for the elevator.

Dylan eyed her with those sexy bedroom eyes. "I missed you, sunshine. So I wrapped things up as soon as I could and hopped the first flight back."

She warmed at his sentiment. "I missed you too." The words came out more easily than she would have thought.

The elevator door opened. No sooner had they stepped inside than Olivia found herself against the wall, held in place by Dylan's strong thighs and his hands on either side of her head.

Instead of kissing her, he dipped his head and settled his lips on her neck, on the sensitive skin behind her ear. His breath was warm, and he grazed her flesh lightly with his teeth.

"Mmm." Her knees buckled under the delicious assault.

He threaded his hands through her hair and tugged, tipping her head and sealing his lips over hers. He kissed her like he'd missed her, kissed her like he couldn't get enough, his big body pressing into hers, his erection a promise of good things to come later.

And she kissed him back the same way until the elevator door opened. He grasped her hand and pulled her out, ignoring the disapproving looks from the older couple waiting to step inside.

Dylan already had a gift in his trunk for his niece but had guessed correctly that Olivia would want to buy a present herself. She found it incredibly thoughtful of him. So after a short trip to the toy store and another to a bakery, this time at Olivia's request, Dylan drove them out to Weston, where his sister lived.

She glanced out the window, watching the trees as they passed. "So give me details before I meet your family," Olivia said, curious about everyone.

"Just what I already told you. Callie is two years older than me. She used to work in retail before she decided to stay home with Ava. She's four now, as you know by the age section of the toy store." He grinned at the mention of his niece. "She's a real cutie. You're going to love her."

Olivia swallowed hard. And smiled. "I adore Ian and Riley's little girl," she murmured, thinking of her sweet niece. But every time she held the baby, now a toddler, the powdery, soft smell reminded her of what she'd lost . . . and might never have again.

She cleared her throat. "And Callie's husband? What's he like?"

"Matthew? He's good to my sister, which is all that matters to me. He works in finance, and he's a great dad."

"They sound like the perfect family."

He shrugged. "If there is such a thing, I suppose they are."

"Do you think there is?" she asked. "I wondered that a lot. Or at least I did after my father's second family was exposed. But I watch Ian and Alex with their wives, and I think . . . maybe it can happen after all." Too bad she was so afraid of believing.

Dylan pulled onto his sister's street. She was the last house on a cul-de-sac in a typical suburban development. He and Callie had grown up in a one-bedroom apartment on a shitty side of Miami. To know his sister had this life meant everything to him.

"You haven't answered my question," Olivia said.

"Not yet, I haven't." He glanced over in time to see her narrow her gaze.

He chuckled with amusement and turned his attention back to the road, where he knew kids played. But he always had some focus on Olivia. Whether she was thinking or nervously chattering or sleeping, he loved watching her.

When she'd walked out of her bedroom wearing a white halter dress with small pink flowers, her dark hair falling over her shoulders and looking like sunshine . . . it'd been all he could do not to pick her up and walk directly back into her room, lock the door, and drive into her until she couldn't remember her name and was screaming his. The fact that her sister had been there helped temper his desire. Even that kiss in the elevator had barely quenched his thirst. She was so fresh and pretty; she checked every box in a want list he hadn't known he had.

Convincing her she could put her past behind her, and whatever else haunted her beyond her father's betrayal, wouldn't be easy. It couldn't be accomplished in bed alone, although he wouldn't mind tying her up and keeping her in his. Integrating her into his family would be a solid start. He never brought women to meet his sister and niece, and he had no doubt that was something Callie would latch onto and treat Olivia accordingly.

He pulled up in front of the house, a peach-colored ranch with a Spanish-styled roof, and parked before turning toward Olivia. He wanted to see her face when he answered her question. "Do I think there's such a thing as a perfect family?" He held her soft gaze as he answered. "I guess I have to believe."

"And why is that?" she asked, eyes wide, and if he had to put a name to the expression on her face, he'd say . . . *hopeful.*

He intended to do everything he could to keep that hope alive. He reached over and tugged on a long strand of her hair. "Because if I didn't believe, there would be no point in being with you."

She opened her mouth to speak, but he placed his hand beneath her chin and closed it.

"I believe we have a barbecue to go to," he said, not wanting her to overthink. "Ready?" He shut the car off and unhooked his seat belt.

She was out of the car before he could open the door for her, and she met him by the trunk. He pulled out the large box from him, and she picked up her gift, which the store had wrapped for her.

"Care to tell me what's in there?" she asked, eyeing the overly large gift.

He grinned. "Oh, only something my sister is going to lecture me over buying too soon."

She laughed at the glee he was sure she saw in his face. "You're a good uncle."

"I try to be. So . . . ready to go meet the troops?"

She drew a deep breath, and he knew she was nervous.

"Ready as I'll ever be."

Her words confirmed it, so he grasped her hand and pulled her in for a kiss on those hot lips, long enough to calm her but short enough not to get caught making out by the car. When he pulled back, Olivia's eyes were glazed, and a smile lifted her lips.

Mission accomplished, he thought and led her toward the front door.

A pretty woman greeted Olivia and Dylan at the front door. "I'm so glad you're here! I missed you, little brother."

Olivia did her best not to laugh, because Dylan was so much taller than his sister, who was even shorter than Olivia's five foot four inches. Like her brother, she had dark-brown hair and pretty brown eyes surrounded by thick lashes. And she wore a casual sundress, which made Olivia feel comfortable with her own choice (well, actually, Avery's choice).

"You must be Olivia," the other woman said. "I was so glad when Dylan left a message he'd be bringing a friend. I'm Callie."

"It's really nice to meet you," Olivia said. "I appreciate you letting me crash your family party."

"The more the merrier. Come out back. We're set up outside."

Company consisted of a princess jumping castle and screaming, happy children bouncing around, high on sugar and having fun. It also consisted of parents running ragged, keeping an eye on their kids . . . or trying to. Olivia sat on the patio along with the adults without rug rat responsibilities. Dylan sat beside her along with his sister and her husband, Matthew, a sweet man with a slightly receding hairline but good-looking nonetheless. They were currently enjoying a break from watching the birthday girl, since she sat on her uncle Dylan's lap.

The little girl was a precious four-year-old who clearly adored her uncle. Even now, the dark-haired imp clapped her hands and chattered as he listened to her with an indulgent smile. A smile that devastated Olivia on a soul-deep level. The man loved children. And she was coming to love him.

No, she forced herself to admit silently, she did love him. She loved the man who wanted her, had gone after her and worn down her resistance until she'd faced the fact that she wanted him too. She'd tried to keep things light. Knew no good could come of letting him in. She sniffed back tears. Happy? Unhappy? She didn't know which, because the revelation had sent her reeling.

Somehow she kept a smile on her face.

"So, Olivia, how do you work with my brother without wanting to strangle him?" Callie asked with a grin that made her look very much like her sibling.

"Who said I don't?" Olivia laughed, grateful for the distraction.

"Ooh, the women are ganging up on me," Dylan said without a hint of fear. "Are you going to help them, Ava?" he asked, tickling her until she screamed, a blood-curdling shriek of glee only a child could manage.

"Dylan, stop!" Callie yelled at him. "She's had more cake and candy than I want to think about. If she gets sick, you're cleaning it up!" Callie stood and held out her arms.

Dylan whispered something in the little girl's ear before standing and handing her over to her mother.

"Potty break," Callie muttered and placed her daughter on her feet and led her into the house.

"What did you say to her?" Olivia asked him.

"I told her mommies are spoilsports and uncles aren't."

"You did not!" She smacked his arm playfully.

"No, I told her we'd play more later." Dylan grinned.

"You love kids, huh?" Olivia asked, hoping she kept the sadness from her voice.

He nodded.

"I can tell." Too bad there was a part of her that was petrified to think of having a family.

Getting pregnant, trying to carry beyond the first trimester, coming to love the unborn fetus inside her body only to lose what she loved . . . and she always seemed to lose. She'd lost her father, if she'd ever had him, and she'd lost the other man she'd trusted after him.

And Dylan? She wondered if she'd lose him too. Eventually.

She pushed those thoughts out of her head. She was enjoying Dylan and his family and Callie's neighbors and friends. Olivia helped her hostess pick up stray plates and cups and brought them into the kitchen.

She held a large plastic bag open wide so Callie could pack it full, and together, they finished tossing the last of this round of garbage.

"I'm so sorry I'm late," a woman said, rushing into the kitchen, sounding out of breath.

Olivia turned her head to see a pretty woman with light-brown hair and a warm smile place a wrapped gift on the kitchen counter.

"Meg! I'm so glad you could make it. And I'm sure Ava will be really happy to see you too."

Meg? Olivia's stomach churned in reaction to the name. Coincidence? Probably not, since Dylan mentioned Meg was like family. Olivia hadn't realized exactly what that meant before now.

Callie hugged the petite woman before turning to Olivia. "Olivia, meet Meg Thompson. Meg, this is Olivia Dare. Dylan's . . ." Callie's voice trailed off as the awkwardness of the situation obviously hit her.

"Girlfriend," Olivia said, finishing Callie's sentence. The word slipped quickly and easily off her tongue, surprising Olivia with how right it felt.

"I'm so happy to meet you," Meg said. "I've heard so much about you." She smiled, and Olivia didn't catch a hint of insincerity from her.

"It's nice to meet you too," Olivia said, trying not to let old insecurities infringe on her now. Dylan, unlike her college boyfriend, had given her no reason to be jealous of or suspect something was going on with his ex. It was only her own doubts that intruded.

"I'm going to run out and say hi to Ava and give her her present. I'll catch up with you in a bit," Meg said and, with a wave, headed out the sliding glass doors to the backyard.

Callie turned to face Olivia. "I'm sorry."

"Why? You have a right to invite whoever you want to your daughter's party. Besides, if Dylan and Meg are friends, I was bound to meet her eventually."

Callie lowered herself into a kitchen chair. "I have to rest my feet for a minute. Join me," she said with a tone like Dylan's that said she expected Olivia to listen.

Olivia dutifully settled into a chair. "You don't owe me an explanation," she told his sister.

"I know but . . . I had an ex-girlfriend situation with Matthew, and I should have been more sensitive. It's just that Meg and I remained friendly. And since Dylan never brings girlfriends to meet us, when he mentioned you were coming, I got so excited that I forgot all about telling him Meg would be here too." She bit her lip. "It's just that I know if I were in your position, I would have appreciated a heads-up."

Olivia really liked Dylan's sister, and she was grateful that she cared enough to explain. "I appreciate you telling me all that." Especially the part about Dylan not bringing other women around his family before her. That little revelation caused a distinct warmth in her heart.

Callie nodded. "Look, I love Meg, but she can be needy when it comes to Dylan, and he's never given her a reason not to be. There's nothing between them but friendship, but she turns to him whenever she has a problem."

"I noticed that," Olivia said wryly.

"I've been there with Matthew, except his ex wasn't as nice and unthreatening as Meg. I had to let him know, in no uncertain terms, it was her or me."

"I've been there too," Olivia said, finding it easy to talk to Dylan's sister. "Except my ex lied about them being just friends, and I was too young and blind to let myself see it. Until I walked in on them."

Callie winced. "That sucks."

More than the other woman knew. "I'm trying to understand Meg and Dylan's relationship, but it's been really hard," she found herself admitting.

Callie leaned in closer. "Listen, I had to push the issue with Matthew and force him to choose. I don't think that will happen with Meg. She just needs to see firsthand where you stand in Dylan's life."

Olivia nodded. "Thank you," she said with feeling.

Callie rose. "You obviously make my brother happy. I want that to continue."

Olivia's throat grew full at Callie's words. She hoped she made Dylan happy. More than anything, she hoped she could continue to do so.

They headed back outside, and Callie was immediately distracted by Ava's shriek. She made a beeline for the jumping castle. Olivia glanced around the pretty backyard and found Dylan in a private conversation with Meg in a secluded corner of the yard.

Olivia's stomach cramped at the sight of their two heads so close together, and she swallowed hard. She might want to be an adult about all this, but that didn't mean she wasn't jealous or worried. She couldn't help it, and she wouldn't apologize for the feeling.

In the past, she might have run, but she decided to listen to Callie's wise words. Meg might consider Dylan her friend, but Olivia intended to make it clear that she was his *girlfriend*. Yes, she thought, that was exactly what she was. Dylan had pushed for them to get serious, and watching him with Meg reinforced her own feelings. So if either one of them had a problem with her staking a subtle claim, she was better off finding out now rather than being blindsided later.

She rubbed her hands together and started across the lawn.

Chapter Nine

ylan shouldn't have been shocked when Meg walked in late to the party. His ex and his sister had remained good friends throughout the years. But he hadn't given Meg a second thought. His only concern had been to introduce Olivia to his family. Now he had them both in one place.

Since Olivia was inside with his sister, Dylan figured now was the perfect time to tell Meg to tread carefully. Olivia needed to understand their friendship, and Meg needed to be aware of Olivia's concerns about his relationship with his ex. He wasn't stupid. He knew Meg relied on him more than was healthy, but he'd never had a reason to call her on it before Olivia had entered his life.

Unfortunately, before he could corner Meg with his own agenda, she'd asked him if they could talk privately for a few minutes about something important. He hoped he had a chance to say what he needed to as well.

She pulled him to a distant corner of the yard, where nobody could overhear.

"Meg, I really need to get back. What's going on?" he asked impatiently. Though he needed to talk to her, this crazy secrecy wasn't what he was after.

"Well, you already know Mike was pissed when he finally came back from Vegas and I had his bags packed and waiting in the front hall, right?"

Dylan nodded. "Yeah. And I told you he deserved to end up on the street and to forget about him."

"I'm afraid that won't be so easy," she whispered.

He narrowed his gaze. "Why is that?" If Meg had let that bastard move back in . . .

"I'm pregnant."

He blinked, stunned at her words, which took a moment to sink in. "What?" he yelled at her.

"Shh! And you obviously heard me." She smiled at him through watery eyes.

He ran a hand through his hair. "Jesus, Meg."

"It's okay," she said, surprising him.

He narrowed his gaze. "It is?"

She nodded, sounding stronger than he'd have expected. "I kinda suspected it, so I've had time to think and make some decisions."

"Did you tell him?"

She shook her head. "I need to. I know that. But throwing him out was hard enough. I couldn't drop this on him too. But I will, not that I expect or want any help from him." She rubbed her bare arms with her hands.

"So you're going to keep the baby?" he asked.

Her eyes opened wide with horror. "I would never give up my own child! Or do anything else like . . ." She shook her head, unable to even finish the thought.

He drew in a deep breath, nodding. "You're going to be a great mom, Meg. You're warm, caring . . . and a teacher. You know exactly what a child needs."

Her face brightened at his compliment. "I think so. I mean, it wasn't planned, and it won't be easy, but I can do this." She placed a hand over her stomach, and her smile was genuine and warm.

Relief at her attitude washed over him. She'd obviously given this thought and was emotionally settled with the idea. "You seem at peace with this, and I'm happy for you."

"Thank you. I'm still scared, but I'm good. I'll have the summer off anyway. I'll find a babysitter and figure it out."

"I know you will," he said, proud of her.

"Can I just get a small hug?" She stepped into him before he could reply, and he pulled her into a brief embrace.

"Excuse me."

Dylan jumped at the sound of Olivia's voice.

Shit, shit, shit. He grappled for an explanation, but he couldn't begin to come up with the right way to justify what, once again, was just friendship. Even he knew it had looked like much more. If he'd seen her ex with his arms around her, he probably would have taken a swing at the man.

"Am I interrupting something?" Olivia asked in a cool voice, her gaze steady on Meg.

"It's not—" Dylan began.

"What it looks like," Olivia said, finishing his lame sentence. "I know. Or at least I hope I do."

"Oh God." Meg stepped up to her. "I know how it must look, but I was just telling Dylan I'm pregnant, and he was congratulating me. That's all."

"Pregnant?" Olivia asked, her shock as obvious as Dylan's had been.

"Yep. By my ex." Meg braced her hands on her still-flat stomach.

"Umm, congratulations?" Olivia said uncertainly.

"Thank you." Meg smiled at her. "Look, I know we just met—"

"You met?" Dylan asked, surprised.

"In the kitchen, when I walked in," Meg explained. "Callie introduced us."

Dylan raised an eyebrow. "You knew I was here with Olivia, and you asked me for a hug anyway? Come on, Meg. That's just all kinds of wrong."

She stepped back, stunned. "I'm sorry. I didn't think—"

"And that's what I wanted to talk to you about, but you told me about the pregnancy first, and I didn't get a chance. You do need to think more. About the kind of guys you get involved with and about me in general."

Olivia grasped his arm. "Dylan, not now, okay?"

He glanced at Meg, who looked sad and small after his outburst. "I'm sorry, okay? I just don't want to be pulled between the two of you. And I don't want to have to make a choice, but if I do—"

"Dylan!" Olivia tugged harder. "It's okay. We both get it now."

He looked from Olivia to Meg, who nodded. "She's right. We do. I need to stand on my own two feet and stop treating you like my boyfriend who's at my beck and call," she said in a low voice. "I just got used to you not being in a relationship at all." She met Olivia's gaze. "I'm sorry."

To Olivia's credit, she smiled warmly at Meg. "Thank you. I'm sorry too."

"Why?" Meg asked.

"Because I've been a bitch about you to Dylan, and that put him in an awkward situation."

Meg blinked at the admission.

He managed a half laugh, half cough. He wasn't used to having such rational, reasonable women surrounding him, he thought wryly. Not that he hadn't understood where Olivia was coming from, because he had. But this détente was much simpler.

"Well, now that that's settled . . ." he said.

"I'm going to get a glass of orange juice," Meg muttered. Obviously embarrassed, she started to walk away.

"Meg?"

The other woman turned.

"I look forward to getting to know you better," Olivia said, surprising the hell out of Dylan.

And if Meg's expression was anything to go by, she was shocked too. "I'd like that."

Meg turned and walked away, and Dylan breathed out a relieved stream of air.

He turned to Olivia. "You're incredible," he said, slipping his arms around her waist.

"Thank you. But I'm reserving judgment on everything."

"What does that mean?" he asked.

"I hated what I saw." She wrinkled her nose. "I mean, I *hated* seeing you two alone in a corner, Meg's arms wrapped around you like you were hers."

He knew better than to crack a jealousy joke or even mention how relieved he was to know she cared enough to *be* jealous.

"If you hadn't read her the riot act, I'm not sure I'd have been able to be civil to either one of you, no matter what I promised myself I'd do or say."

He slipped his hand around her ass, making sure her back faced away from the party and toward the woods behind the house. Then he pulled her into him, letting her feel how much he wanted her. "This is for you. Got that? And only you."

Her stiffness melted out of her, her body softening against his. "I know that. And hearing you stand up for us? That meant the world." Her voice cracked, and right then she stole another piece of his heart.

"You do realize Meg is going to need you even more now, right?" Olivia asked.

He shook his head. "She's an adult, and she will have to learn to stand on her own two feet and make the right decisions. Especially now. I'm her friend, but I'm not her husband, boyfriend, or anything like it. I'm yours."

"Okay then." Olivia smiled.

He nodded. "Okay then." He hoped Olivia meant what she said and that everything between them was fine.

The party wound down, Ava opened her overly expensive American Girl doll that she loved, and soon Olivia and Dylan said good-bye to everyone and left his sister's house. Meg had gone home awhile before, claiming she wasn't feeling well. Olivia didn't want her sick, but she also didn't want her embarrassed or upset. She just wanted peace, and she hoped she would eventually get along with Dylan's ex. He didn't mention Meg, and Olivia was smart enough to let the situation go.

Instead, she wanted to go home with her man. Her man. That was what Dylan was, at least for now. She didn't know what the future held, but she did know she'd have to tell him everything about her past. She couldn't tell herself she loved him and hold the most vulnerable parts of herself back. Even if the words had never been said between them, even if she wasn't sure just how deep he was really in . . . after all, he'd said a lot of words, none of them *the* word, but she owed him the truth.

They arrived back at his place, a luxury apartment a block away from the ocean. "I've never been here before," she said, glancing around.

"I know. And as soon as I'm finished with you, I'll give you a tour. Not that there's much to see." He grinned and wrapped an arm around her waist, pulling her close. "Except in the bedroom. There's plenty to see in there." He picked her up and swung her into his arms.

"Dylan!" She laughed at his impulsive move. She ran her hand up and down his cheek. "I need to talk to you," she said.

He groaned. "Before or after?" He did her favorite move, nuzzling her neck, making it perfectly clear what he would prefer to do now.

"Now," she said, despite the fact that her entire body was humming with sexual need.

He tipped his head against hers and groaned. "Okay. But not in the bedroom. I won't be able to concentrate if I have you on my bed." He turned and walked back to the den and deposited her on the sofa, coming down beside her.

He clasped his hand around hers, as if sensing she needed strength for whatever it was she had to tell him.

"Remember I told you that my college boyfriend cheated on me?"

He nodded. "If this is about Meg—"

"It isn't," she rushed to assure him. "It's about me, but to tell you all of it, I need to start at the beginning."

"Okay then. I'm listening."

She blew out a long breath. "Okay, well, I guess it all starts at home. Because when I look back at that relationship, I should have known he wasn't fully engaged. All the signs were there, but I chose to ignore them because it was easier than facing it. And where did I learn that from?" She met Dylan's understanding gaze before continuing. "My mother made the avoidance of truth an art form."

"Your father and his other family." Dylan stated the obvious. "You think she knew?"

Olivia shrugged. "I didn't realize it then, but I was a kid. My mom? She had to have at least sensed that those long, extended business trips were something more. He missed holidays, birthdays, *their anniversaries...*" She shook her head. "Don't get me wrong. She was ... She *is* a great mother, but she had to have known my father wasn't faithful."

Dylan stroked her cheek. "I'm sure you're right. And I see how that affected you. On many levels."

"Well, it's learned behavior, that's for sure. So I ignored so much of what Jeff did; I accepted his excuses because I'd watched my mother do the same. It never dawned on me to question. Not then, anyway." She gnawed on her lower lip.

Maybe on some level, she'd deliberately picked out a guy like her father, one who was full of himself and his own needs.

"That's a huge revelation for you," Dylan said. "But you have to know I would never cheat—"

"I know." She placed her finger over his lips. If she didn't get everything out now, she didn't know if she'd find the courage again.

He playfully licked, then nipped at her finger, and she moaned softly. "Later," she murmured, despite the wetness now dampening her underwear.

He grinned and nodded. "I'll behave."

"Just for a little while. Then you can be as bad as you want." She swallowed hard, hoping he'd still want to be bad when he heard not only about her past but about how it made her feel now.

"Okay, let's do this. What else do you need to tell me?" he asked.

"I walked in on them together, which is how I found out."

"I remember you telling me that," he said with anger in his dark eyes.

Anger for her, and it filled her with emotions she'd never experienced before. Warmth and happiness all rolled into one package.

Now she just had to get through what came next.

Dylan waited—outwardly patient, inwardly not so much—for Olivia to talk to him. Whatever she had to say, she believed it would change the course of their relationship. And it had him on edge.

"There was a reason I went to find him that day." Her hand curled tighter around his. "I was pregnant, and I had to let him know."

"Jesus." She'd been so young.

"And you already know what I found him doing."

"Another woman," he said with disgust, wanting her to feel his support.

"His teaching assistant. Best friend. The same woman who he always had to reassure me that there was nothing going on between them."

Dylan swore. No wonder she had such a visceral reaction to his relationship with Meg.

"I caught them in the act and ran out. But later, when I did tell him about the baby, he blamed me. As if I'd gotten myself pregnant." Tears dripped from her eyes, and she angrily wiped them away.

"Want my shirt?" He lifted the bottom of his tee for her.

She shook her head and smiled. "Thanks, but I'm okay."

He grabbed hold of her other hand too. "What happened to the baby?" he asked softly.

A huge shudder went through her small frame. "For you to understand, you need to get where my head was at."

"I'm here. I'm listening. For as long as it takes."

"I didn't tell anyone at school, but when I went home on vacation, I told my mother, and she promised to be there, whatever I decided."

"She sounds great."

"She was. She still is. She was willing to discuss all options. I wasn't sure what I wanted at first, but I knew I had a limited window to decide. I was petrified. If I kept the baby, I'd have to drop out of school, and who knew if I'd ever be able to go back. I'd be a single mother with no viable career . . ."

Dylan couldn't imagine what it must have been like for her back then. "You were so strong," he said.

"I didn't feel strong. I was so scared, but even then I couldn't bring myself to think about having an abortion, and before I knew it, I had gotten through the first trimester of the pregnancy. And then I started to feel the baby kick." Her eyes lit up at the memory. "And then I started to consider what having a baby would mean. A little life dependent on me. Someone to take care of, who would love me."

Understanding went off in Dylan's head. There lay the crux of the story. He knew Olivia well enough to understand that her issues stemmed from the fact that her father, the first man in her life, had essentially abandoned her. A father was supposed to love his child unconditionally. Instead, Robert Dare had put another family, other children, above his first wife and kids, above Olivia. Then the father of her baby had done the same thing at a time when she'd barely been an adult herself.

"What happened?" he asked.

She drew a shuddering breath. "No sooner had I made peace with the decision than it was over. I woke up one night, and there was blood everywhere." She shrugged, her voice cracking. "I miscarried. And that little person who was supposed to be mine to love was gone. I didn't realize how much I wanted the baby until that blood was everywhere."

A shudder went through Olivia, followed by tears and small gulps as she struggled to pull herself together. All Dylan could do was hold her tight and be there until she finally wiped her eyes and sat up straighter, meeting his gaze.

"I'm so sorry, honey."

She nodded. "Thank you."

"I'm glad you shared that with me."

She forced a smile, and he could tell it was forced. "The thing is, losing the baby scarred me. It defined me. And I really don't know if I can let myself feel that kind of pain ever again."

"What are you saying?"

"I was depressed for so long afterward and . . . I'm not sure I ever want to get pregnant again."

Dylan's head buzzed at her words. The emotional part of him, the part that had always expected to have a family one day, rebelled against every word she was saying. He'd grown up without a father or mother to speak of, and he wanted the life he'd been denied. Hell, he wanted it with Olivia.

"I saw you with Ava today, and I'm sure you want kids some-day. I thought you should know where my head is before this thing between us goes any further," she said, her voice thick as she stared at him, hands folded in her lap, eyes wide and expectant as she waited.

Waited for him to walk away. Because she'd never had a man stick by her before, he realized with shocking clarity. Thanks to her past, she didn't trust that she was important, that she was enough to keep any man in her life.

But she was. For him, she was everything.

The reality sucker-punched him, but thank God he real-ized it in time. Of course, it was a risk to stay, to continue to invest himself when she clearly believed what she was say-ing. That was why she'd insulated herself from relationships for so long and why she'd fought against *them* every step of the way.

And this? This was just another means of pushing him away before he left her in the end. That was how she thought. What she believed. Which meant it was up to him to prove her wrong.

He turned toward her, clasping both of her hands in his. "Okay," he said at last, speaking into the heavy silence.

She wrinkled her nose in confusion. "Okay what?"

"Okay, I understand. You don't think you want kids. So let me ask you something. When did I ever say I was in this relationship for any reason other than you?"

Eyes glassy, she narrowed her gaze. "You don't mean that."

"Are you calling me a liar?" he asked, his voice dropping in warning.

Her lips parted, but he didn't want to hear another word out of her mouth unless she was screaming his name while he was pounding hard inside her.

So he rose and pulled her with him, heading straight for the bedroom, where he could begin to show her he wasn't going anywhere. He'd just have to dig in, be patient, and wrap her in all the love and security she'd never had, hoping that eventually she'd trust in him and in them enough to change her mind. And want the family he intended to have. With her.

It was the biggest gamble of his life.

Chapter Ten

Olivia's office had been a revolving door with people coming in and out all day. She was busier than ever, and for that, she was grateful. Because whenever she had down time, her thoughts turned to Dylan. So now, she sat at her desk, fingers playing with the sun pendant around her neck, a constant memory of the great guy she had in her life. She'd told Dylan the truth about her past and her fears about the future, and he hadn't left.

No, he was still here with her, and she didn't know what to make of that. How could he not care that she wasn't certain she wanted children? How could he think *she* was enough? Sure, he might believe that now, but wouldn't he come to resent her later?

A full workweek had passed, and nothing between them had changed except he'd stepped up his pursuit, as if trying to prove a point. He'd sent flowers to work, taken her out for dinner or cooked for her at his apartment, and she'd ended up sleeping there every night. If his goal was to convince her that he wasn't going anywhere, he was doing a damned good job.

In fact, they'd fallen into a routine that she could easily get used to. If only she could relax and let herself believe everything would be okay, but instead, she tossed and turned each night. She was exhausted in the mornings, and not even a double dose of caffeine helped.

She wasn't surprised when a knock sounded on her office door. It had been that kind of day.

"Come in!" she called out, looking up. To Olivia's surprise, Meg entered, shutting the door behind her.

She was wearing a pair of black slacks with dust and paint stains that told her she'd probably come straight from teaching her kindergarten class.

Olivia rose, but Meg gestured for her to sit. "I'm sorry to just show up like this."

"That's okay. Are you here to see Dylan?" Because Olivia couldn't imagine why Meg would be here to visit with her.

Meg shook her head. "I used his name as a way to get past the gate though. He has me on his approved list. But I really wanted to talk to you. I was hoping you'd still be here."

"I wish I wasn't," Olivia said, then realizing how that sounded, she shook her head. "I meant, it's been a long week, and I'd rather be home than at work."

Meg stepped into the room. "I get that, believe me."

Olivia gestured to one of the chairs on the other side of her desk, and Meg settled herself in with a groan. "I am exhausted. This first trimester is rough."

"I—" Olivia had been about to say, *I remember*, but caught herself in time. Dylan might know, but she wasn't about to confide in a stranger. "I understand. So what can I do for you?" she asked.

"You mean why am I here?" Meg smiled ruefully. "I felt really bad about what happened at Dylan's sister's house. When I looked at things from your perspective, I realized that I wasn't being fair." She drew a deep breath. "I guess I got used to having Dylan at my beck and call. As a friend," she was quick to follow up, her cheeks turning a healthy pink in embarrassment.

Olivia was uncomfortable as well, but she respected the fact that Meg had come here to face her.

"But that's all Dylan and I are. And as his friend, I want him to be happy, and you obviously do that for him so . . . I'm sorry." Meg seemed to run out of words at the same time she ran out of breath. She might've rushed her confession, but she really seemed to have a good heart.

"I appreciate you coming by," Olivia said, certain it couldn't have been easy.

"I just want you to know that I won't call Dylan all the time. I'll make that break. But I would like us to try to be friends?"

Olivia smiled. "I'd like that. Because I know Dylan doesn't want to lose you." And Olivia understood that, or was trying to. She had so many brothers and sisters. Dylan had one. Meg made two, if she believed them both, and she wanted to—in a healthy way. Not in a dysfunctional, not-seeing-the-obvious kind of way.

"Thanks for saying that." Meg rose to her feet. "Well, I'm sure you want to get home, and I have a long weekend ahead of me. If the baby's father calls me back, I still need to tell him that I'm pregnant."

Olivia winced. "Oh, wow. Good luck with that. Do you think he'll take it well?"

"Doubtful," Meg said with a shake of her head. "He's an immature child. I really have to learn to pick better men," she muttered. "Of course, now I'd have to find a man willing to take on crazy me and my child. In other words, it's just going to be me and the peanut." She patted her still-flat stomach.

Olivia blinked, realizing just how much she understood Meg's predicament. She'd found herself in a similar position a long time ago. Way too similar. But nothing that had happened to Olivia, from the cheating ex to losing her baby, would help Meg to learn now. So Olivia remained silent, despite her crazy impulse to confide in the other woman . . . a woman who was open and friendly and easy to talk to.

"Good luck," Olivia said.

"Thank you. And thanks for seeing me. And being so understanding. Maybe we can grab lunch on one of my rare days off? Or on a weekend," Meg said in one of her rushed statements.

"I'd like that," Olivia said, meaning it. She reached into her desk and pulled out a business card and scribbled her cell number on the back. "Call me."

Meg treated her to a genuinely warm smile. "Thank you."

Olivia rose and walked Meg to the door, opening it only to find her sister-in-law, Madison, on the other side.

Meg walked out, and Madison walked in. "God, this day is crazy. It's been one meeting after another."

"Want me to come back another time?" Madison asked.

"No! I always have time for you." Olivia gave her a hug. "You look fantastic." She stepped back and took in Madison's long blonde hair and glowing cheeks. "I take it my brother's still treating you right?"

Over time, it had become easy to refer to her half siblings the same way she did her full-blood ones. They weren't to blame for her father's actions, and she really did like Alex and the rest.

Madison nodded. "Yes, he is. Marriage has been good for him. For us."

"I just wish you hadn't eloped. We all wanted to be there for you."

Madison met Olivia's gaze. "I know. But without any family to speak of, I just wanted it to be Alex and me. I didn't want to feel like I was walking down the aisle alone, you know?"

Olivia understood. Madison had grown up in foster care and had deep abandonment issues that Alex had had a tough time overcoming. Then again, considering he'd dumped her once, he'd deserved to have to work hard for his second chance.

"Our family is your family. You know that, right? And there's a lot of us," she reminded her brother's wife.

Madison nodded, her blue eyes filled with grateful tears. "I'm good now. It was just the idea of the wedding and all those traditions I didn't want to deal with. But going forward? I'm all in with you Dares."

Olivia laughed and hugged her sister-in-law again. She released her and gestured to the chairs.

"Want to sit?"

Madison nodded, and they both settled into the seats in front of Olivia's desk. "I'm really here to fill you in on Marcus." Madison ran the new educational seminars and program Ian had instituted for players to learn how to function postfootball career. She had been a social worker first, treating Riley after a bad run-in with her abusive father, which was how Alex had met her.

"How is he doing?" Olivia asked. "I haven't seen or heard from him since the Pro Bowl."

Madison raised her shoulders and lowered them again. "On the one hand, he's willing to do whatever we ask of him. He's started working with the financial counselor, and he's agreed to let us sign him up to talk at colleges about the difficulties of turning pro."

"That sounds really positive, right?"

Madison nodded. "But I've been meeting with him about breaking ties with bad influences in his life, and he's really torn up about sending his cousin home. His family is giving him a hard time."

Olivia blew out a frustrated breath. "I can't imagine his parents wanting him around someone who's a problem."

"I don't know. I just know he's still susceptible to the man, and that could be an issue. I hope he stays away."

"Got it," she said glumly, wanting Big to be a success in more areas of his life than just on the field.

"All we can do is give him the tools to fix his life. The rest is up to him. You're doing all you can for him. We all are."

She nodded. "I know. Thanks for letting me know."

"So how are things with you and Dylan?" Madison asked.

Although Olivia shouldn't have been surprised by the question, she wasn't prepared to dig into her own feelings. "We're good," she said as she rose and headed back behind her desk.

"Oh really? Then why did you just beat a hasty retreat behind your desk?" the onetime social worker asked.

Olivia rolled her eyes. "It's really annoying that you're analyzing me."

Madison shook her head and laughed. "I'm doing no such thing. I walked in here, took one look at you, knew you looked exhausted and that something's bothering you. I call it friendship, not analysis." She folded her arms across her chest and eyed Olivia with a knowing but determined gaze.

Olivia let out a sigh. "I appreciate that you care. I just have some things I need to work out in my head."

"Fine, but don't let those things keep you from a good man. I nearly did that, and it was a serious mistake." Madison rose to her feet. "And if you need anything, make sure you pick up the phone."

"I will." Olivia knew how fortunate she was to have family and friends who cared, unlike Meg, who seemed like she was alone. And if anyone knew what that was like, it was Olivia.

Dylan met Olivia downstairs by the exit to the parking lot at five o'clock as planned. Sexy as ever in a black skirt that hit above her knee and loose silk shirt with a subtle V-neck that provided a hint of cleavage, he could look at her all day without getting bored. It was enough to make his mouth water and his body perk up despite the long day he'd had.

"So what do you want to do tonight?" he asked as they walked to their separate cars.

She liked having her car, and as long as he had her, he didn't mind. "I could make reservations at Emilio's," he said of a small, intimate restaurant near Alex's apartment.

"Would you mind if we didn't go out tonight?" She hid a yawn behind her hand. "I'm so tired—I would kill to go home, change into comfortable clothes, and order in pizza."

"As long as home is my place," he said, sliding his hand into hers.

She glanced at him for a long moment, and he thought she might change her mind, but she nodded. "Sounds good. I just need to stop home for a few things."

"I'll order, and it'll be there by the time you arrive."

"You rock." She leaned in and kissed him on the lips.

He grasped her waist and pulled her close, sliding his tongue into her mouth and making up for the full day's absence. He swirled his tongue against hers, teasing her with his teeth and lips until her knees went weak, and he was satisfied she'd think about nothing but him until she got home. And it *was* home.

He slowly released her mouth and rubbed his nose against hers. "That ought to hold me over until later," he murmured.

A little while later, they ate pizza while discussing the situation about Marcus. Dylan filled her in on his day, and she did the same. He appreciated the daily intimacies they'd begun sharing and hoped she felt the same way.

They'd finished their pizza and had settled in each other's arms on the sofa. He inhaled the floral scent of her shampoo that he'd become familiar with and slid his hand beneath her shirt, settling his palm against the smooth skin of her belly.

"I had a visitor today," she said. "Meg came by the office."

His hand stilled. "You're kidding. What did she want?" Because if she'd upset the delicate balance he was walking with Olivia . . .

"She was sweet. She said she was sorry about how things looked on Sunday and that she was used to having you at her beck and call. But she wouldn't put you in that position again."

"How did you feel about it?" he asked, holding his breath, hoping this didn't lead to a problem.

Olivia shrugged in his arms. "I appreciated it. I think it took a lot for her to come see me, and I believe she was sincere."

He blew out a long breath. "For what it's worth, I do too."

"She wants to get together for lunch sometime."

Now *that* Dylan wasn't sure about. Those two women together would either make his life easier or give him another uphill battle with Olivia.

"I said okay." She rolled to the side so she could meet his gaze. "I know she's important to you. Like Callie's important to you. So I can be an adult. I want to give something to you for once."

His chest grew heavy at her words. "Liv—"

"Shh." She shut him up by crawling into his lap and sealing her lips over his.

Her tongue slipped into his mouth, her body adjusted to his, and he was lost. In her kiss, he felt everything she didn't— couldn't—say. Her silken tongue slid against his, over and over, until her hips were rolling against him in time to the rhythm she set.

He groaned and cupped her head in his hand, holding her in place so he could taste her more thoroughly, more deeply. He couldn't get enough of just this simple kiss.

Her small hands gripped his shoulders as she rocked her sex against his aching cock, which demanded he strip her and thrust into her waiting warmth. But he wasn't in the frame of mind to take more just yet, not when *this* was so damned good.

He continued to kiss her, to make out like he hadn't done since he was a teen, when the ringing of a cell phone intruded on the perfect moment.

She lifted her head, and he felt the loss of her lips on his.

"It's mine, and I say ignore it," she said.

Good by him. Whoever it was could take a flying leap.

He slid his hands around her waist, needing to touch her skin, and nuzzled his face into the side of her cheek. "You smell so damned good, it makes me hard just breathing you in."

She moaned and nipped at his lips. They continued their lazy kissing, Liv arching and rocking into him, her sex hitting his pubic bone with every subtle move she made.

"Dylan, God, I could come just like this." Her fingers pinched his shoulders through the soft cotton of his shirt.

"Then do it, baby."

She arched her back and rolled her hips, pressing her sex into his groin, her breath coming in short pants until she stiffened and groaned, riding against him to completion. It was so incredibly sexy, such a turn-on that his own release was building, but no way was he coming in his pants. He was saving that pleasure for the minute he thrust inside her.

She fell against him, sated, and he wrapped his arms around her. They breathed together until she shifted and met his gaze.

"Your turn," she said, her eyes heavy-lidded, her lips well kissed.

"I'm not going to argue, except you'll be coming again along with me."

His hands touched the hem of her shirt when her cell rang again. She narrowed her gaze. "Let me get rid of whoever it is." She scrambled off him, grabbing her purse and digging for the phone.

She glanced at the cell screen. "Marcus," she mouthed to him.

She answered, sitting down beside Dylan again and tipping the phone so they both could hear. "Marcus, what's up?" she asked.

"Miss Olivia, I need you."

"Where are you?" she asked.

"Home." His voice dropped. "Just come over."

"What's wrong?"

Silence followed.

"Marcus, what's going on?" Olivia asked, sounding worried.

Dylan grabbed the phone. "Marcus, it's Dylan Rhodes. What's wrong?"

The other man's words weren't coherent, and even Dylan grew worried about the slurred mess. "I'm on my way," Dylan said and hung up, all thoughts of sex with Olivia receding from his brain.

"*We're* on our way," Olivia said in a firm voice. "Do not think you're going without me, Dylan. Marcus called me and—"

He shut her up by sealing his mouth over hers, his tongue thrusting inside. He slid his hand behind her head and tugged her back. "Liv?"

"Hmm?" she asked, dazed but obviously very much aware of what was going on.

"I was going to say okay, let's go together."

A flush rushed to her cheeks. "I just assumed—"

"I don't want you to get hurt, but I know damned well you'd just follow me there. Now are you ready?"

She nodded.

Dylan made it to Marcus's house in record time. If there'd been a cop on the road, he'd have definitely been pulled over, but someone was looking out for him. He pulled to a stop by the curb. The huge house Marcus had bought after he'd signed his big contract loomed in front of them.

Dylan grasped Olivia's hand in his, holding on tight as he led the way. The front door was ajar, and when a noise sounded from inside, Dylan shoved the door open farther and stepped into the dimly lit foyer, Olivia by his side.

"Marcus?" Dylan called.

Without warning, the lights flicked on, nearly blinding him with their intensity, and he blinked to adjust his sight. And without warning, Olivia screamed as her hand pulled out of his.

One minute Olivia's hand was warm and secure in Dylan's; the next, she was pulled against a hard body.

She jerked away, but whoever had her held on tight.

"Don't move," Wendell said, shoving a gun into her side. Behind her, his wiry frame was hot and sweaty. Olivia's mouth ran dry, and fear rushed through her.

"You son of a bitch," Dylan said, facing Wendell.

"Where is Marcus?" she asked, hoping the other man was okay and could somehow help them.

"In the kitchen. I asked him to call and get you here, and he did."

Marcus had set them up? Olivia thought she might get sick.

"He's a good little cousin—or he was until *you* got in the way." Wendell prodded her harder with the weapon.

She winced, and Dylan took a step forward.

"Stay back! I've got the bitch *and* the gun."

Dylan came to an immediate halt, his hands raised.

Olivia tried to think if she could get herself out of this without anyone being hurt. Drop to the floor? He'd shoot Dylan. Kick into him? Again, he had the gun. Frustration along with dread washed over her again.

"Wendell, put the gun down," Dylan said in a deceptively calm voice. "You don't want to get yourself in more trouble with the cops."

"I won't get in any trouble. Marcus will. *He* called her. He got you both here. Drugged and at gunpoint. But nobody knows that except me."

Olivia breathed out a relieved sigh that Marcus hadn't deliberately led them here. "Where is he?"

"I put something in his drink, and he's passed out cold. So when they find you two shot, nobody will question who did it."

Dylan sucked in a breath. "Why would you frame your family member?" he asked in an obvious attempt, at least to Olivia, to keep the man talking.

"What family? Marcus stopped treating me like family. He cut me off and told me to go home. I shoulda been the one to make it big. I was a better player than he ever was till I got hurt. It shoulda been me!"

A familiar refrain. Marcus had obviously heard it enough to believe it. She wondered if Wendell had ever taken responsibility for anything that had gone wrong in his life.

"And it's all *her* fault. She put him in those classes. She thinks he can make his own decisions. I'm sick and tired of hearing about what Miss Olivia said," Wendell muttered, his tone biting. "She and Marcus are both gonna pay. And since you're here, so are you," he spat at Dylan.

The gun dug into her ribs painfully, but she held her reaction in, not wanting Dylan to lose his temper and end up being the one hurt.

"I'm sure Marcus would still help you with money, even if you couldn't be here with him in person," Olivia said, trying to reason with Wendell.

"Shut up! You know that's not true."

"This makes no sense, Wendell. Think, man. You can still get out of here before you do something you can't take back," Dylan said. His hands were raised in the air, but he attempted a step toward Wendell.

He twisted the gun in her side, and she gasped loudly, her eyes tearing from the pain.

"Why should I just give up? I got nothing, and I should have had everything. My cousin made it big in the NFL, and I had access to the good life until *she* interfered and told him to get rid of me. Then she hooked him up with dumb-ass financial classes and people who told him to look out for users. Now he thinks I'm one of them."

Dylan held her gaze. She didn't trust him not to try to save her at his own expense.

"Who the fuck asked you to interfere? Any of you?" Wendell continued his tirade, his voice wild, the gun digging deeper, bruising her skin.

She swallowed past the pain. "Maybe if you hadn't caused Marcus and the team unwanted publicity, we wouldn't have had to get involved," she said, trying to explain and force him to be reasonable.

"This was supposed to be easy!" Wendell ignored her, ranting like a spoiled child.

A spoiled child with a deadly weapon.

"You can still get what you want," Dylan said to the man. "Marcus can send money home, and you can be the big man there."

"Even I know there's no fun in being the big man in East Bumfuck," Wendell muttered. "I'm done talking to you." He raised his gun and aimed it at Dylan, as if Wendell knew he'd have to go through Dylan before taking out Olivia.

"No!" she screamed, hoping to distract Wendell.

Just then, the sound of a loud roar echoed through the house. A huge body came flying forward, slamming into Wendell, tackling him, and knocking Olivia sideways against the nearby closet door.

She glanced over in time to see Marcus slam his fist into Wendell's jaw with a sickening crack.

"Freeze!" Dylan yelled, standing over both men with Wendell's gun in his hand, which he must have retrieved from the floor.

Marcus rolled off his cousin and held up his hands, looking more like an overgrown kid than a man.

Suddenly sirens rang out in the air.

"I called the cops," Marcus said, slumping against the nearest wall.

Wendell started to rise, but Dylan leveled the weapon at him. "Just give me a fucking reason."

The police burst through the door, guns drawn. Dylan immediately dropped his weapon and raised his hands in the air.

Olivia remained curled around herself as the cops sorted through what had happened, until finally they checked Dylan's ID, confirmed the story with Olivia and Marcus, and snapped cuffs on Wendell, who'd skipped bail in Arizona and had a warrant out for his arrest.

No sooner had they released Dylan from questioning than he pulled her up and into his arms, her entire body shaking. She grabbed on to him and held on as he ran his hand over her hair and down her back, keeping her pressed tightly to him.

Chapter Eleven

By the time Dylan brought Olivia back to his place, he was ready to jump out of his skin. The presence of the police at Marcus Bigsby's house was on the news in no time, and the rest of the story spread just as quickly. Television news crews and paparazzi showed up before Dylan and Olivia had been released by the police. Eventually the cops led them out a back door and escorted them to Dylan's, where he fielded calls from Ian and the team's PR team while Olivia took a long, hot shower, to—in her words—wipe the stench of Wendell off her body.

He was in shock from how quickly the events of the night had gone down. One minute they'd been ready to make love here, in his apartment; the next, she'd been held at gunpoint, and Dylan's life had completely flashed before his eyes. A life without her in it—and it hadn't been worth living.

He stripped to his boxer briefs and crawled onto the bed to wait. Folding his arms behind his head, he stared at the ceiling, forcing himself to stay calm.

A few minutes later, the shower had stopped, and Olivia walked into his bedroom wearing one of his large T-shirts. He loved her wearing his clothes. He loved her, period. Nearly losing her merely confirmed everything he did want with her. Family. Kids. A full, happy life and one she was completely capable of having, if only she'd let go of her fears.

She curled into him, but her phone was full of messages and still ringing with family members checking in. And there were a lot of Dares for her to reassure, starting with Ian and her mother. She reassured each and every person, insisting she was fine and she didn't want company—that she needed to be alone. She'd send him a wink and continue with each call.

She was on her fourth or fifth sibling—Dylan had lost track which—when he realized she was speaking to Avery. These sisters had a dynamic that was easy to recognize, and he grinned as he listened to Olivia volley sarcastic comments in between promising that she'd never been in any real danger. A lie if Dylan had ever heard one. He still shuddered when he thought of Wendell and the gun he had shoved into Olivia's ribs.

"Don't worry," Olivia said. "I promise you I'm fine. It was a freak thing. It won't ever happen again."

He couldn't hear the other side of the conversation, but the sound of her voice soothed him.

"Av?" Olivia paused, then asked, "Did anyone call Dad?"

Dylan stiffened at the obvious tension in her voice as she asked that question.

"Yeah. I know he and Savannah are in LA." Another wait. "No, don't call and tell him. It's fine."

But it wasn't, Dylan thought. For her sake, he wanted to believe her father hadn't yet been told, but he knew from his own parents' lack of caring that anything was possible. And she'd already admitted to him how much her father's betrayal had hurt. It was obvious to him that much of Olivia's insecurity stemmed from her unstable relationship with her father. Dylan understood parent issues all too well considering he didn't have a relationship with either one of his. But his situation had always been the same. One parent had left early in his life, the other later on. And while his mother had been present, she might as well not have been. So all in all, no rug had been pulled out from under Dylan's feet the way it had been for Olivia when she'd found out about her father's other family.

At times like these, he had to wonder if Olivia's issues could be overcome at all . . . but he refused to think that way. He was too invested in her to believe she wouldn't conquer her past.

With a groan, he stretched and closed his eyes. It was late, and it'd been a long day.

Once she hung up with Avery, she moved on to her various other family members, and he enjoyed the different relationships she shared with each. Listening gave him a unique insight into her character, seeing how she spoke to each sibling, full and half, in her life. Did it bother him that he didn't have the same? No, because he had Callie and her husband and daughter. Not as big and boisterous as Olivia's family, but just as overprotective.

"Finally!" Olivia proclaimed and tossed the phone on the bed beside her. "Last call, and I am so sorry."

He smiled. "I don't mind. They obviously love you."

And so do I. He met her gaze, wondering if she could read his unspoken thoughts.

"They do," she whispered, her voice catching. "And if it were any one of them who'd gone through what I did today, I'd want to hear their voices too."

She laid her head in the crook of his shoulder, and he curled his arm around her tightly. "I could have lost you today."

He'd never tasted fear before. Never understood what the phrase meant. Not until she'd had a gun in her gut and a crazy man holding her hostage.

"You weren't exactly safe yourself." Her fingers tightened, biting into his stomach.

He hadn't been worried about himself, only about her. He inhaled her fresh-from-the-shower scent, and his cock hardened. He wanted to press his hand against himself to alleviate the ache, but she'd notice. And he didn't want to pressure her after the day she'd had. But he needed to feel her slick and hot around him and know they were both alive and together.

She ran her fingers back and forth over his abdomen. "I'm not tired," she said in a husky voice. "In fact, I think my adrenaline is still running high."

He blew out a relieved breath. "Thank God."

Without warning, she levered herself up and straddled his waist, a wicked gleam in her eyes. "Glad to see we're on the same page."

"I like you in my clothes." He slid his hand beneath the hem of the oversize shirt he'd lent her only to discover she wasn't wearing panties beneath. He blew out a rough breath. "Jesus, Liv."

She grinned. "Surprised?"

He laughed, but the sound was as strained as his already aching erection. He pushed himself up against the pillows, giving him more leverage to play.

"You know I'm tempted to start here." He slid a finger through her damp folds, and she trembled above him. "But I think I'll tease you instead."

He inched the shirt up over her stomach, sliding the hem higher until he uncovered her breasts. She yanked the tee over her head and tossed it to the floor, leaving her completely nude and his for the taking.

He loved her body, the slender curve of her waist and the small rose-tipped breasts he could hold in one hand. He leaned forward, capturing one rigid nipple between his teeth, pulling on the bud until she threw her head back and groaned.

"And here I thought I was taking control," she said.

He chuckled but kept teasing one nipple with his tongue and teeth, using his fingers on the other breast, pulling and plucking at the sensitive tip until her hips were gyrating in circles over his straining erection. The soft cotton of his boxers provided too much of a barrier to her wet heat. He wanted to feel her sex directly over his cock. Needed her to slide down his shaft so her inner walls pulsed around him.

"Get my boxers off," he said through clenched teeth.

"My pleasure." She slid them down his legs, and he shook them off.

Then Olivia climbed back on top, her knees on either side of his hips, her sex poised over his cock.

"Wait," he managed to grit out.

Her beautiful eyes met his, her lids heavy with desire. "Why?"

"I want you to look at me when you slide down over my cock."

Her lips parted softly. "Oh."

He didn't want this over fast. He wanted her to know how he felt, and he didn't want her to be able to avoid what was between them.

"You wanted to be in charge," he reminded her. "What are you waiting for?" He raised his hips, nudging the blunt head of his cock against her sex.

She moaned and released her leg muscles, gliding downward and cushioning him in wet heat until she was seated completely.

Fucking heaven.

He drew a deep breath and had to remind himself of his own words. He met her gaze. In her eyes, he saw the same overwhelming emotion slamming him inside and out.

Dylan's heart beat hard in his chest. "Take my hands," he said, watching as she clasped her smaller fingers around his, her eyes wide and locked on him.

She raised herself up and down, finding her rhythm and milking him with every move. He lifted his hips, grinding against her and thrusting up every time their bodies met. He might not have wanted fast, but that's what he was getting, and he didn't care. Not since she was right there with him. Soon, her pumping motion changed, and she locked her legs around him, grinding her pelvis into his.

"Oh, Dylan. Oh God." She squeezed his hands so tight, he was sure the blood flow stopped completely.

"That's it, sunshine. I'm with you."

His world narrowed to where their bodies connected and how she held on to his gaze. A buzz reverberated in his head, and wave after wave of ecstasy threatened to take him over. He was going to come, but damned if she wasn't going with him. He released his grip on her hand and reached down, pressing against her clit with his finger.

Her silken walls contracted around him even tighter than before.

She moaned loudly. "Dylan, I'm coming!"

Her words along with the look in her eyes did him in, and he began thrusting upward until he exploded inside her, his hot come pumping out of him as he came hard, feeling more connected to Olivia than ever.

Olivia finally caught her breath after the incredible orgasm that had sent her soaring to heights she'd never felt before. That was Dylan. Each time with him was better than the last. She rolled to her side, and Dylan pulled her back against him, cushioning her in warmth.

"Today scared the shit out of me," he said, whispering into her hair.

She nodded. "Me too."

"Wendell had that gun shoved in *your* ribs, not mine." He squeezed her tighter, as if he was afraid if he let her go, he'd lose her.

She swallowed hard. "But he was going to shoot you first."

Dylan flipped her over and faced her, one arm propping his head up. She looked into his handsome face, the goatee that was so much a part of him, those dark eyes and tanned skin, and her heart flipped over.

"I nearly lost you today, Liv. And that is *not* okay."

The intensity in his voice shook her to her very soul. "I know, but—"

"No buts." He tapped her nose. "I nearly lost you today, and that is not okay because *I love you.*"

All the oxygen departed from her brain, leaving her light-headed and dizzy. It was one thing for her to think it, another thing for him to say it. "Dylan—"

"No running from this," he said, not once breaking eye contact. "You don't have to be ready to say it back, but you need to know how I feel. And know that I believe you feel it too."

She reached out to touch his cheek. "I do." She swallowed hard. Saying the words was so hard because they left her vulnerable. But she realized she was vulnerable just by virtue of the fact that she felt them at all. She loved him, and that left her open to any number of painful outcomes, as she'd experienced firsthand.

But she gathered her courage . . . and with her heart pounding in her chest and her head spinning, she told him what was in her heart. "I love you too."

He grinned, that panty-melting grin that could make her do almost anything. "Yeah, sunshine. I thought so. Now here's the thing."

She narrowed her gaze, not liking that serious tone of voice. "What?"

"We didn't use a condom."

She reared back, shocked that she, of all people, hadn't realized that herself. "Oh shit." Her heart began pounding painfully inside her chest. "I'm not on any other kind of protection."

She'd never needed it. The times she'd had sex, she'd made sure her partners used a condom. She was religious about it and for good reason.

"What is it about you that makes me lose my head?" Dylan said as she inched back to her side of the bed only to find herself jerked forward and pulled close, her face inches from his. "Don't panic."

"Didn't you hear me the other day? I don't want to go through anything like losing a baby ever again!"

"Sunshine, you're jumping the gun. I'm sorry neither one of us realized in time, but I promise you that if you're pregnant, this time, you won't be alone. You have me."

Nausea threatened at the word *pregnant*. She didn't hear anything else, couldn't see past it. "Dylan, I told you how I felt about kids, and you said—"

"I know what you told me. I even know you believe you don't want children. But that's fear talking." He stared at her pointedly. "That's your past talking. That's the little girl whose father was never, ever around, who doesn't want to be hurt again. Left again. That's *her* talking."

She wasn't just talking—she was screaming, Olivia thought, reminding herself of how badly it hurt when everything fell apart.

"Hey. Stay with me," Dylan said, pulling her back to the present. To him. "It's also the young woman who lost both a baby and a man who should have been there for her taking. But it's not who you are today," he said, that steady, so-sure gaze never leaving hers.

"I thought you understood. You said you did. And you said I was enough for you," she said, her voice rising.

"I did understand. I still do. And I didn't lie to you, though I admit I hoped you'd come to see you wanted the same things I did," he admitted in a gruff voice. "I didn't do this on purpose, but honestly? Today with Wendell made me realize that life is short. And it merely solidified what I've always known. I want it all. A house, white picket fence, dog, kids, all of it. With you," he said in a determined voice.

She struggled to sit up, pulling the covers with her and covering her bare breasts, feeling completely exposed and a lot betrayed. "A lie by omission? I hate to break it to you, but it's still a lie."

He sat up just as quickly and grabbed her wrists before she could climb out of bed. "A lie based on hope. And faith. And a belief in the woman I've come to know. The one who could accept Meg's offer to be friends. You know that woman? I had faith in her. I still do."

"What are you saying?" Olivia asked, complete panic swamping her. "If I don't agree, if I don't want those things, you'll leave me?" She hated how her voice cracked, betraying her emotions.

He shook his head, a wry smile tugging at his lips. "You'd like that, wouldn't you? If I walked out on you, you'd be able to tell yourself that, once again, you weren't enough. And you'll crawl right back into the shell I found you in and never come out. So no, Liv. I'm not going anywhere. And news flash. Neither are you."

She blinked at his determined tone of voice.

"Pregnant or not, you're going to work through your issues, and I'm going to be there when you do." He raised an eyebrow, challenging her to argue.

She couldn't do anything except collapse on the bed and cry, the stress of the day, the release of adrenaline, and all the pent-up emotion she'd been holding in for days pouring out. True to his word, Dylan was there, holding her until she fell asleep.

The next day at work, chaos descended, leaving Olivia with no time to think about Dylan, a possible pregnancy, or the future. Apparently, Olivia being held at gunpoint by Marcus Bigsby's cousin made for sensational news. The PR team needed her to do interviews, which meant fast media training and prep. She was fed a quick diet of talking points and taught how to answer a question by changing the direction to what she wanted to focus on—which was the need for the team to support Marcus, for Marcus to focus on cutting bad influences from his life, and getting ready for the next season.

Since she really didn't enjoy being in front of the cameras, she appreciated the training. Even better, since she wasn't the face of the team, Ian instructed PR to choose one interviewer. The other networks could pick up clips afterward. Having her older brother in charge was a perk Olivia appreciated.

She wasn't surprised when, later that day, as soon as she was free, Ian called her to his office. She walked down the

Hall of Fame, as the hallway, lined with large framed pictures of their most talented players, was known. The photos always made her smile. She liked feeling like she was a part of history, that the men they worked with were making an impact on the sport.

She reached Ian's office, knocked, and strode inside. Her brother sat behind his big desk, looking every inch the intimidating team owner he was.

To her, he was just her big brother. "What's up?"

He held out his arms, and with a grin, she walked to him for a huge hug. "You took ten years off my life," he muttered.

"If that actually happened every time you've used the expression, you wouldn't still be here." She squeezed him back. "I'm fine." She stepped back and settled onto the couch in his office.

He joined her, taking the closest chair.

"How's Big doing?" she asked.

"The kid's shaken up. When the cops are finished with him, he's going to go home for a while. And when he returns for training, he's going to learn how to function in the real world."

Olivia nodded in agreement. "I hope this incident helped him see the light. That not all people are good, even if they are family."

Ian nodded. "And that's enough business. How are *you*?"

She plastered a smile on her face. "I'm fine," she said, getting tired of the expression that was nothing more than a lie. She twisted her fingers together in her lap and thought about Dylan's ultimatum that wasn't.

"You're great, huh? That's why your smile's forced? Why you're practically breaking your fingers?" Ian pointed to her intertwined hands and let out a low growl of frustration. "Do I need to kick Rhodes's ass?"

"No!"

"Then whose?" her big brother asked.

"Mine," she said, looking away.

He shifted to the couch, sitting close beside her. "Hey." He lifted her chin with one finger. "What gives?"

She shrugged. "Dylan said he loves me. And I love him." Her voice cracked as she spoke. "But he wants everything, and I don't know if I have that in me to give." No way would she mention not using a condom to her brother. *That* would be TMI.

Ian gave her his patented big-brother, reassuring smile. "History. You're afraid it's going to repeat itself. I ought to know. But Dylan isn't Dad. And he isn't Jeff. You can't lump all men together."

She smiled. "No, not all men. I had you and Scott. You were always there for me. But . . ."

"Dad wasn't."

"Right. Speaking of the devil, he's been calling all morning."

"Did you talk to him?" Ian asked.

She shook her head. "I know it's weird, since I'm the one who forces everyone to go to his parties and to make nice, but he always shows up a day late. Like we're—or I'm—an afterthought."

And Olivia had a love-hate relationship with him. On the one hand, she'd been upset last night when he was the only one who hadn't reached out to check on her. And on the other hand, she'd avoided his calls today, when he'd been trying to contact her. The man couldn't win, but then that was the nature of her conflict with him. She sighed.

"I'm not Dad's biggest fan—you know that," Ian said.

She nodded. Of all their father's legitimate children, Ian had taken their father's betrayal the hardest. Or so it seemed. Olivia always tried to play nice, hoping for crumbs. Ian had all but frozen their father out.

"I get you, Liv. You still want the family you never had, and you want Dad to be . . . Dad. There's nothing wrong with that. But deep down, you know you aren't going to get that from *him*."

She nodded, the lump in her throat painful. "I do know that. You're right."

"Always," he said with a grin.

She shrugged. "I know Dylan isn't Dad. Dylan is . . . He's perfect, and I still can't move on completely."

Ian let out a laugh. "I hate to break it to you, but no one's perfect. Especially not Rhodes."

She chuckled at that. "Fine. But you know what I mean."

"Let me ask you something. If Mr. Hero is so perfect, why are you so afraid he'll disappoint you?"

Damn, her brother always knew just where to zero in.

Ian cleared his throat. "That's not what's really bothering you. It's what Dylan wants from you. And you haven't really dealt with the fallout of losing a baby so young," Ian said, speaking gently.

She balled her hands into tight fists and swallowed hard; the tears started flowing at just the *mention* of the baby. She hadn't dealt with it well. Or at all. She'd seen a psychiatrist once, and she hadn't gone back. Because the pain of it all had been easier to suppress than feel.

"One day, I felt the first flutters in my belly." She pressed her hands to her stomach hard. "Then I lost the baby, and with it, I lost the ability to believe in anyone or anything." Tears streamed down her face unchecked.

And poor Ian, who never knew what to do with one of his crying sisters, sat helplessly. But he listened, and she loved him for it.

"You haven't lost it, Liv. You just need to be brave. Don't shut down on Dylan now. Work through everything you have to before you blow a chance at real happiness. Because even a good guy like Dylan can only take so much."

She flung her arms around Ian's neck and hugged him tight. "I love you, you know."

"I love you too." He squeezed her back. "Now get back to work," he said gruffly.

She stuck her tongue out at him playfully. "You hate it when one of us girls gets mushy."

"So when are you coming over to see your niece?" he asked, taking her off guard.

Olivia tipped her head guiltily. That was something else she avoided, spending too much time with young kids. Even her brother's child. She resisted the urge to touch her stomach. It was too soon to wonder. Too soon for any of this. "I'll come by soon. I promise."

Ian pinned her with a steady gaze. "I'm going to hold you to that."

She nodded. "I'd expect nothing less." She ducked her head and left, taking her time walking back to her office.

No sooner had she returned to her desk than the phone on her desk rang. "Hello? Olivia Dare speaking."

"Olivia, it's your father."

She closed her eyes and drew in a deep breath. She should have expected him to try her desk when he couldn't reach her cell. "Hi, Dad."

"Hi, Dad? You're threatened by a man with a gun, and all you have to say to me is 'hi, Dad'?"

She pressed her phone to her temple before putting it back to her ear. "Who told you?" she asked, glad he'd finally called despite it all.

"Well, let's see. First Alex, then Jason, and eventually Sienna. They called me in LA."

But none of her full siblings had alerted him, and Olivia wasn't surprised. "I didn't realize you were out of town."

"It was a spur-of-the-moment decision. Savannah and I needed time away, so we took a nice, long vacation. Didn't I call you before we left?"

"No, you didn't." She drew a deep breath for courage, because confronting him had never been easy. "You forgot my birthday, you know."

The silence that followed was awkward and uncomfortable. Finally he cleared his throat. "Didn't Savannah's . . . I mean, our gift arrive?" he asked.

"No." She glanced around the office she'd decorated with pictures of her favorite Thunder players on the wall, plants on the windowsill, and photos of her siblings on her desk. Those were the people who cared.

"Olivia, I'm sorry. I know Savannah sent a present. I'll have to have her check and see why it didn't arrive."

She blew out a frustrated breath. She believed her step-mother had sent her something. She liked her father's second wife despite the circumstances. It wasn't about material things. It never had been.

"It's not the gift I care about," she explained. "It's the fact that you missed my party and you didn't call ahead of time to let me know." And she'd always been the stupid daughter who made excuses for him to the rest of her siblings. *Why?*

"I do tend to screw up with you kids, don't I?" he asked, sounding low and defeated.

But she wouldn't feel bad for him. She couldn't. Not when he'd made her feel worse. Tears burned her eyes, and she opened the bottom drawer in her desk, where she kept a box of tissues.

Damn the man, she hated crying at work for any reason. She blotted her eyes and leaned back in the chair. "It's fine. I have to go. I have a lot of work to catch up with. Bye, Dad." She hung up without waiting for him to reply.

Somehow Olivia survived the long week of fending off the media, and she wanted nothing more than to spend the upcoming weekend doing nothing. Except nothing wouldn't help her life.

So she drew a deep breath and made a list of things she would be able to do, things she needed to face in order to move forward. She hoped she could handle it. Because the risk of what she could lose if she didn't was so very great.

Chapter Twelve

ylan let himself into his sister's house, knowing it was just around bewitching time for Ava. Sure enough, the munchkin was attempting to avoid brushing her teeth by hiding behind the living room curtains.

"It's not hide-and-seek time," Callie called out to her daughter.

"Yes, it is!" came the reply.

Callie met Dylan's gaze and grinned. "The good news is she doesn't realize she can't talk back to me while playing hide-and-seek and still . . . hide." Callie tiptoed into the family room and swept her daughter into her arms, curtains and all.

Ava shrieked, then caught sight of him. "Uncle Dylan!" Another piercing scream, her flailing arms held out wide.

Dylan caught her easily. "How about I help you brush your teeth and tuck you in afterward, and then you promise to go to sleep, hmm?"

"Yay! Teeth!" She waved her little hands in the air.

Callie clenched her jaw. "I hate it when she does a one-eighty for you."

"And you love it at the same time, because she is going to bed." He swung her over his shoulders and headed up the stairs.

A half hour and a lot of water splashing and storytelling later, Dylan had tucked Ava into bed. Twice. She came out three more times, and his sister handled things until she finally settled in for good.

Callie groaned from the big club chair in the family room. "Business trips really do suck," she muttered. "I'm glad you're here."

Dylan laughed. "I'm sure Matthew misses you as much as you miss him."

"I'm sure he's enjoying his night alone in a quiet hotel," she said wryly. "But he'll be home tomorrow, and Ava's bedtime duties are all his."

"Teamwork."

Callie's head picked up at the tone of his voice. He hadn't meant to be so revealing, but the bedtime ritual with Ava had hit him square in the chest. What he'd never had growing up. What he wanted going forward. And who he wanted it with.

"Dylan, what's going on? What's wrong?" Callie asked, concerned.

His sister had always been able to read his moods well and vice versa. He knew it had more to do with how they'd raised each other than the normal sibling bond.

"Is everything okay with Olivia? Because I really liked her," Callie said.

He smiled. "She liked you too."

"So what'd you do to screw it up?" his sister asked.

Dylan rolled his eyes at her conclusion. "I told her I loved her and wanted a life with her. How's that for a screw-up?"

"Oh. Wow."

He shoved his hands in his pants and paced the small room. "I thought we had it rough, right? Dad bailed, Mom eventually did the same. We had each other . . . but we coped, right? We want to have the life neither of us had growing up. Hell, Call, I don't want to be on the outside looking in anymore. Looking at the families and love other people have and wishing I had it for myself."

Had he forgotten a condom on purpose? *Hell no,* he thought. There was no way he'd put Olivia through such emotional anguish and torture because of his own selfish needs. But would he be sorry if the end result was a baby? *No,* he thought. He wouldn't. But she might be, and that scared the crap out of him.

His sister rose and walked over, wrapping her arms around him as she'd done when they were kids. "If Olivia doesn't want that with you, she's a stupid woman."

He loved how she stood up for him. "I think she wants it. But she's petrified of having it—and losing it. Again." He explained about how Olivia had grown up with just her mother home, the blow with her father's other family, then the pregnancy and cheating boyfriend and subsequent loss of her baby.

"Oh, that poor girl."

"Yeah. But she's not that girl anymore. And I want her to see that."

Callie stepped back. "If she's as smart as I think she is, she'll come around. I know that's not much to go on . . ."

He laughed, the sound hollow. "But it's all I've got. Trust me, I know."

"Are you seeing her tonight?"

Dylan shook his head. "I wanted to come here, and she promised her sister she'd go see a movie. I think a little separation is good. Healthy." Something he might need to get used to if she decided not to fight for them.

Olivia followed the directions to the address that Madison had given her. A medical building on the nice side of town. The psychologist Madison recommended, someone she thought would mesh well with Olivia's personality and needs. That made her laugh since Olivia didn't know what she needed. She only knew what she couldn't afford to lose.

She'd told Dylan she was going to the movies with Avery because she had a feeling she'd need time alone after this appointment. If she wanted to get past the fear of losing every good thing that came into her life, if she wanted to have the life he envisioned, she was going to need help. The help she'd walked away from years ago.

A little over an hour later, she walked out of the same building, eyes red, feeling completely drained. The older doctor was warm but direct, expecting Olivia to answer questions and be honest. The doctor warned her that therapy took a while, change didn't happen overnight, and she'd have to be willing to do the work in order to get past the emotional barriers she'd put up to block her own happiness.

And when Olivia had explained that she might not have time because she could, in fact, be pregnant now, the doctor assured her there was always time. And Olivia supposed that was true.

She climbed into her car, exhausted but aware of one thing. She'd taken that difficult first step. Regardless of what happened with Dylan, she knew now she had to do this for herself most of all.

Before she started up her car, she checked her cell. Avery had left a message, and Olivia played it back. Apparently Avery's first love, lead guitarist for the famous rock band Tangled Royal, was back in town for a concert. He'd taken off and made it big. He'd wanted Avery to go with him, but ever since her younger sister had donated bone marrow and had been forced to face Sienna's cancer at a young age, Avery had a need to remain around her family. Instead of taking off with him, she'd nursed a broken heart, which had always made Olivia sad for her vibrant, outgoing sister.

As far as Olivia knew, Avery hadn't seen or heard from Grey Kingston since he'd left town. But since he was famous, good-looking, and splashed all over the tabloids, it was impossible not to be aware of his every move.

Avery had offered up two tickets, one for Olivia and one for Dylan. Beneath the offer and the bravado, Olivia sensed Avery's need for her older sister, and she intended to be there for her sibling. And a concert would keep Olivia busy and surrounded by people, as opposed to being alone with Dylan, her thoughts and the words of her new therapist crowding in on her.

The next morning, Olivia asked Dylan's secretary to let her know when he arrived at work. When she got the call, she headed right over and knocked on his open office door.

His eyes opened wide, pleasure washing over his face at the sight of her. He rose to his feet. "Morning," he said in a husky voice.

"Morning." Her pulse picked up speed at the sight of him.

"Shut the door," he said.

She automatically did as he asked.

"Now lock it."

"What?" She blinked at his second command.

"I haven't seen you since yesterday, and you're here now . . . so lock the door."

Her heart skipped a beat at his commanding tone. "Dylan . . ."

"Olivia . . ."

"Fine." She flicked the lock closed and strode toward him, one purpose in mind. "I'm here to invite you to a concert tonight. With me and Avery."

He tipped his head to one side, studying her. "Tonight works fine for me. Now come here." He crooked a finger her way.

She rolled her eyes. "What's with the orders?"

He waited until she was within arm's reach and snagged her around the waist, pulling her close. "Last time I saw you was yesterday, and I want a few minutes alone with you. Is that such a bad thing?"

She shook her head. "No, I just—"

"If I asked nicely, we'd still be arguing over what I wanted and why."

The man had a point. She was on the defensive.

He braced his hands on her shoulders and lowered her until she sat on his desk. "How are you?"

She shrugged. "Okay."

"No, you're not. But you will be," he said with more confidence than she felt. "Just be yourself with me. Everything else will fall into place."

She blew out a long breath. "I hope you're right." She hesitated, then blurted out, "I'm trying to work on things. On me. I just don't want to have to worry about long, brutal discussions each time we're alone," she said, opting for honesty.

"Me neither." He kissed one side of her mouth, then the other. "Is that what the concert is about? A way to keep from having to talk?"

She blushed at being called out. "That's a side benefit," she admitted. "But the truth is, the lead guitarist is an old boyfriend of Avery's, and this is the first time she'll be seeing him since he left her. She doesn't want to go alone." She shrugged. "And I don't want to go without you."

He lifted her up and placed her on his desk, ignoring the papers he set her on. "That's music to my ears. Get it? Concert? Music?"

She rolled her eyes. "Someone is in a good, if silly, mood."

"You're here. Of course I'm in a good mood."

She sighed. How could she resist this irresistible, persistent man? "Okay, well, the concert starts at eight, and Avery has backstage passes for all of us afterward."

He slid his hands around her waist and pressed a warm kiss to her lips. "Trust me," he whispered before lifting her off the desk, turning her around, and sending her back to work with a pat on the ass.

She grinned for the rest of the morning, knowing that had probably been his intent.

Avery was a bouncing, hyper mess throughout the concert, Dylan thought. Whoever this guy was, the normally unflappable sister looked like she was about to jump out of her skin. But the concert itself was spectacular, as were their seats. Clearly these weren't bought on the Internet. Avery must have been sent these tickets, but according to Olivia, she didn't want to discuss it. She just wanted physical and moral support, which Olivia was all too happy to provide, and Dylan was happy to be along for the ride.

The closer they got to the end of the concert, the paler and the more obviously nervous Avery became. More than once, Olivia pulled away from Dylan and leaned into her sister, whispering in her ear. Placing an arm around her shoulder and squeezing her tight with reassurance and love.

He liked the relationship between Olivia and her siblings, because from the teasing to the protectiveness, it reminded Dylan of himself and Callie. And he understood from watching Olivia with her sister just how much love and caring she had to give.

The band walked off the stage, and the crowd went crazy, chanting for an encore. They were treated to two more rounds of music before it became obvious that the band wasn't returning. The lights flickered on, and people began to gather their things, getting ready to file out.

Dylan's cell vibrated, and he pulled it out of his pocket and looked. Meg's number flashed. He shot Olivia a look, but she was busy talking to Avery.

"Hello?" Dylan asked.

Whatever Meg wanted to say, the noise in the arena and the bad reception prevented him from hearing. He frowned and shoved his phone back into his back pocket.

"Who was it?" Olivia asked.

"Meg." He watched her with a wary gaze.

"Everything okay?" she asked.

He shrugged. "I couldn't hear. I'll call her back outside the arena later on." He glanced at his watch. It was after eleven p.m., and by the time they finished backstage, it might be too late for him to call.

"Do you want to go find a place with service?" Olivia asked.

She didn't sound disturbed or concerned by Meg calling. Maybe she was making progress with things, Dylan thought.

They finally made it through the long aisle of seats, up the row, and exited through the big doors. Vendors were packing up shirts but still selling to willing customers. He shook his head. "It's fine."

A niggling feeling in his gut bothered him, but he pushed it aside.

Olivia slid her hand into her sister's, and they followed her to the nearest security guard. She flashed a guest pass and asked where they should go.

"This way." Avery pointed in the opposite direction.

"Hey, are you sure you want to do this?" Olivia asked.

Avery nodded. "Except . . . I think I'm going to go alone."

"What?" Olivia shook her head. "No. If it's awkward or he's got groupies hanging all over him, you may need me."

Avery faced her sister with a forced smile. "I love you for coming this far with me. You kept me calm while I waited. But this is something I need to do myself. But thanks for reminding me of the groupies. That was a reality check I could have lived without." She winked at Olivia.

"Oh God, I'm sorry, Av—"

Dylan stepped up. "Do you want us to walk you wherever you need to go?" he asked Avery.

She drew a deep breath and shook her head. "Nope. Again, I'm going to do this myself. But thank you. Really."

"How will you get home?" Olivia asked.

"I'll get Uber. Don't worry."

"Okay. Text me so I know you're home safe, or I swear I am calling 911."

"Okay, Mom," Avery said with a groan.

Avery hugged her sister and kissed Dylan on the cheek. "You two go on. I'll fill you in tomorrow."

Since Olivia seemed about to argue, Dylan grasped her hand and tugged. Avery seemed set on her decision. "Come on. She can handle it."

With a sigh, Olivia nodded, and Avery strode off. "He's probably a spoiled rock star," she muttered.

"And Avery is an adult who can judge for herself."

"Fine."

He clasped her hand, and they wound their way out of the arena. When they hit the humid Florida air, he pulled out his phone. Olivia did the same.

"Meg called me too," she said. "I'd turned off my phone."

"How does she have your number?" he asked.

"I gave it to her when she came to see me."

Dylan hit redial, knowing if she'd tried to reach Olivia as well as him, something was wrong. He met Olivia's wide-eyed gaze, shaking his head when the call went to voice mail.

"Have you spoken to her recently?" Olivia asked in a soft voice.

He shook his head. "I think I was a little rough on her at my sister's. She hasn't been in touch." He'd planned on calling, but he'd been overwhelmed with worry for Olivia, and he'd forgotten. He winced at that.

"When I saw her that day? At my office? She was waiting for her ex to call her back so she could tell him about the baby. She didn't think he'd take it well. Do you think something could have happened?"

"Shit," he muttered. "The guy's a lazy ass, but I didn't think he'd hurt her." He tried her again as they walked to the car.

Finally, on the drive back to Dylan's, his cell rang. It wasn't Meg, but he answered quickly through the Bluetooth speaker in his car. "Hello?"

"May I speak to Dylan Rhodes?"

"Speaking."

"Umm, my name is Lana Santos. I'm Meg Thompson's neighbor."

Dylan tensed, and Olivia gasped and leaned forward in her seat.

"What's wrong?" he asked.

"I got your name from her cell; you were her ICE number."

"ICE?" he repeated, unclear what she meant.

"In case of emergency," the other woman explained. "After the ambulance left, I realized her phone was still on the floor."

"Ambulance?" Dylan asked, his voice rising. He shot Olivia a concerned glance. One look said she was as worried as he was, and he wished this woman would get to the damned point.

"I'm not sure what happened, but she had an argument with that man who used to live with her. I heard yelling. Something crashed—"

Dylan gripped the steering wheel so hard his hands hurt. "What hospital?" he asked, interrupting the woman.

"University of Miami, I believe."

"Thank you for calling," he said, disconnecting. Dammit, he should have known that bastard might lose it when he heard Meg was pregnant.

"Breathe," Olivia said, her soft hand on his thigh and her voice a surprise. He'd been lost in his own thoughts and panic. "You need to stay calm."

"Yeah," he said, knowing she was right.

He took the nearest exit and changed directions, heading to the big hospital.

Olivia focused on keeping Dylan calm, but by the time he pulled into the hospital parking lot, Olivia was in a panic of her own, feeding off his silent nervous energy and her own concern over Meg.

For a myriad of reasons, Olivia hated hospitals. The white walls, the cold personnel, the antiseptic smell all worked to bring back memories, none of them good. Some involved visiting Sienna once she'd been allowed to have company after her procedure; others included Olivia's own visit to the ER when she'd lost her baby.

They approached the desk, and he leaned over. "I'm looking for someone who was brought in by ambulance. Meg Thompson."

The woman typed some information into her computer and looked up at him—in her own time. "I'm sorry, what was the name again?"

"Thompson," he said through gritted teeth. "Meg. She was brought in by ambulance."

"Oh. Yes. Are you a relative?" she asked.

"I'm her brother." He squeezed Olivia's hand tighter.

"Through those doors. Someone inside will direct you further."

Dylan pulled Olivia down the hall and through the double doors. They did another *are you a relative* check and were finally directed to a closed-curtained cubicle.

"Maybe I should wait here," Olivia said, speaking softly. "Meg doesn't really know me and—"

He didn't let her finish. He merely pushed his way around the curtain, again pulling Olivia along with him.

Chapter Thirteen

Meg lay in the narrow bed, her head propped up, her eyes closed, face pale.

"Meg?" Dylan spoke her name.

Her eyes fluttered open. She took one look at Dylan and burst into tears. He stepped closer and eased into a chair by the bed.

"How did you know I was here?" she asked, sniffling as she pulled away.

"Your neighbor found your cell and called your emergency contact." He met her gaze. "Let's start with the most important thing. Are you okay? Is the baby?"

"I'm okay. The baby is too . . . for now. I'm bleeding, so they have me on bed rest, and they're monitoring me."

Olivia's stomach cramped, and she took a step back, toward the curtain and the exit.

"Thank you for coming." She glanced at Dylan, then raised her gaze to Olivia, acknowledging her with a grateful smile.

Meg didn't seem to mind that she was there, but for Olivia, this was all way too close to home.

"What happened?" Dylan asked.

She drew a shuddering breath. "Mike finally called me back. I asked him to come over because we needed to talk. I had to tell him about the baby."

Dylan nodded. "And?"

"I'm not sure, but he might have been drunk. He definitely was off from the minute he walked in. I just wanted to get it over with, and he just . . . exploded. He accused me of getting pregnant on purpose to trap him. Which is ridiculous. I mean, he wasn't someone I wanted to keep and—"

"What did he do?"

Olivia heard the steel beneath the question, the simmering anger.

"He grabbed my wrist, told me that he wasn't paying a fucking dime. I said fine. I didn't want anything from him anyway. I told him I expected him to sign away any legal rights to the baby." Meg blinked back tears. "He said I had to prove it was his first."

What a bastard, Olivia thought. At least Jeff hadn't questioned paternity. He'd just insisted she get an abortion, she thought, the memory coming back with stabbing, painful clarity. He'd said if she was dumb enough to get pregnant, it wasn't his problem.

"I told him go to fuck himself," Meg said.

"Good for you, Meggie," Dylan said, admiration in his tone.

Olivia agreed, silently applauding her backbone and courage. At nineteen, Olivia hadn't been confident or strong enough to call Jeff the bastard he'd turned out to be. She'd curled in on herself instead. She swallowed over the lump in her throat.

"And then he . . . he released my hand and shoved me hard. I stumbled back, tripped, and hit the curio cabinet with all my grandmother's beautiful antiques." Her voice cracked, and a lone tear slipped down her cheek. "The glass broke, the pieces fell . . . and he just walked out." She swiped at her face with the back of her hand. "I didn't start bleeding till later. And the doctor said it may have had nothing to do with the fall. That it's so early in the pregnancy that it's hard to know these things."

Olivia remembered those words too. *It's hard to know why these things happen, Miss Dare. Sometimes it's just nature's way of handling things.* God, she hated that Meg was going through this. Hated remembering her own past even more.

"But the doctor said everything might still be okay. I just have to rest. And wait."

Olivia hadn't been that fortunate. She'd already lost the baby by the time she'd gotten to the hospital, and they'd had to do a *procedure* to take care of the rest. She winced at the memory.

"That's good," Dylan said, obviously talking about the baby still being okay.

"I want to be a mom," Meg whispered. "I didn't know if it would ever be in my plans, but now that I have the chance, I want this," she said, determination in her tone. "No matter what happens now, I want to make sure the chance doesn't pass me by just because there's no Mr. Right."

"Right now, focus on resting. Everything will fall into place," Dylan told her.

Meg nodded. "I know."

Olivia shook her head, her own thoughts spinning because Meg, having gone through her own ordeal, was still thinking about a future, a baby, no matter what happened now. Amazing.

Quietly, knowing nobody would miss her, Olivia backed out of the cubicle and made her way to a small waiting area and settled herself in a chair. She pulled her legs up and wrapped her arms around them, lost in thought, in Meg's misery combined with optimism, and in her own past.

The room was empty, at least for now, and Olivia was grateful for the privacy. She blew out a breath, feeling the sudden need to talk to someone who loved her and understood. Meg had Dylan, and oddly, she didn't begrudge her that. But she needed someone too.

Normally, she'd call Avery, but her sister was tied up with her own drama at the moment. Olivia loved her mother, but she'd never felt like she understood her choices. She didn't want to bother Ian and Riley, so she dialed her brother Scott.

As a cop, he worked odd and often late hours, so she could count on him to answer the phone.

"Hey, Liv," he said, picking up almost immediately.

"Hi. Are you busy?" she asked.

"Just got off shift. What's up? Everything okay?"

She blew out a long breath. "I guess I just needed to hear a familiar voice."

"Uh-oh. What's going on?" he asked in that brotherly way he had, the one that told her, like Ian, if someone had deliberately hurt her, there'd be hell to pay.

"Well . . ." Scott wasn't as up to date on her love life as Avery, or even Ian, so she summed up her night as best she could. He knew Dylan and had been at her birthday party, so their involvement wasn't a shock. She gave her brother the bare basics about Dylan's friendship with Meg and how they'd ended up here at the University of Miami hospital. "So I left them alone to talk, and I'm sitting here by myself. I—"

Scott cleared his throat. "Listen, Liv. That's pretty damned close to home for you."

"Yeah." Her voice caught, and she realized she was shivering.

"The station's not far from the hospital, and like I said, I just got off duty, so I can be there in ten minutes," he said.

She shook her head. "No, you don't need to come. I just wanted to hear your voice."

"See you in a few, Livvy," he said, using her childhood name. And he hung up before she could argue further.

She tapped her phone against her temple, cursing those domineering Dare genes that the men in her family seemed to have inherited.

True to his word, Scott arrived not long after. He had dark hair like Ian and indigo eyes like hers. He was older than her, younger than Ian, and a rock-solid man, someone she could always rely on.

He walked in, having changed out of his uniform into a pair of jeans and a black tee. He took one look at her and held out his arms.

She stepped into her brother's embrace. "Thank you."

"For not listening when you told me not to come? You're welcome." He pressed a kiss to the top of her head. "I'm sure this is rough for you. Kind of like reliving things?"

"Yes, except . . . I'm on the outside looking in, and suddenly I'm seeing things I never let myself see before."

"Such as?" He grasped her hand and led her to the chairs.

"I've been looking at my future, at my *life*, from the perspective of a nineteen-year-old. Dylan said as much, but I didn't know what he meant. I couldn't *see*."

I even know you believe you don't want children. But . . . that's your past talking. That's the little girl whose father was never, ever around, who doesn't want to be hurt again. Left again . . . It's also the young woman who lost both a baby and a man who should have been there for her talking. But it's not who you are today.

"So what's changed?" Scott asked.

"His friend Meg. She was pushed around by her ex-boyfriend; she's pregnant and hoping she doesn't lose her baby. Yet she realizes even if she loses this baby, she *wants to be a mother one day*." Olivia wiped her damp palms on her jeans and rose.

Scott followed, but he let her pace, let her think.

"That's such an adult thing to say," Olivia murmured. "So wise." She spun back around to face her brother. "And it's not something I would ever let myself feel, because I was thinking with my nineteen-year-old brain and all those pent-up emotions and the hurt from back then. I wouldn't let myself move on."

"Liv, I hope you understand where you're going with this, because I gotta admit, I'm sort of lost."

She grinned. Such a typical man. "That's okay because I'm not. I finally see and understand what I want." Olivia laughed and threw her arms around his neck. "Thank you for listening."

He wrapped his arms around her. "I'm so glad you understand. And you're happy. That's all I want."

Olivia blew out a breath. "That's all I want too."

Dylan knew the minute Olivia stepped out of the room, but he couldn't up and run after her just yet. He shook his head, hating being torn in two. "Did you call the police about Mike?" Dylan asked.

Meg shook her head. "He didn't assault me; he was frustrated and—Don't look at me that way! I'm not making excuses. I don't want that bastard anywhere near me. I had to call 911 when the bleeding wouldn't stop and was so heavy, and the paramedics saw the mess with the cabinet. They asked what happened . . . I had to tell them anyway, in case being shoved impacted the bleeding, so it's all documented."

He frowned, knowing if he saw Mike on the street, he'd knock the other man into next year. "It's not enough."

"They aren't going to arrest him for shoving me once. And considering his reaction, he won't be back. He doesn't want anything to do with me or the baby." She covered her stomach with her hands. "I didn't realize how much I wanted to keep the baby until I saw all that blood and realized I might lose it. All I care about now is holding on to him. Or her."

As Dylan patted Meg's hand, he remembered Olivia saying the same thing when she'd described her ordeal, and for the first time, he realized how hard this night must have been for her too. Hearing Meg's story had to have brought up all those painful memories. The ones she was trying to get past in order to give *them* a future.

He swallowed a curse.

Meg leaned her head back against the pillows, obviously exhausted.

He rose to his feet. "I should let you get some rest."

She nodded. "I'm tired."

He leaned over and kissed her forehead. "I'll come back and check on you soon, okay?"

"Thanks, Dylan. And thank Olivia for me. I'm sorry I interrupted your date."

"Just think about yourself and the baby. It's all good," he told her, hoping he was right.

After leaving Meg, Dylan asked a nurse where he could find the nearest waiting room. He followed the directions, hoping Olivia had gone there and hadn't left the hospital instead.

He heard voices as he approached and paused in the doorway, startled to see Olivia hugging another man, who, when he stepped back, he realized was her brother.

Jesus, he did not need any more shocks or surprises tonight. "Everything okay?" he asked, walking into the stark waiting room. Other than a few plastic chairs and a table with undoubtedly outdated magazines, the room was sparse and empty.

"Fine," Olivia said, meeting his gaze. "I called Scott, and he was in the neighborhood after work, so he stopped by."

Dylan raised an eyebrow. She'd called him to say hello at almost midnight or because she was upset?

Except she didn't seem as upset now as she'd been before.

"Scott," Dylan said, extending his hand.

"Rhodes," Scott muttered. He accepted the handshake.

"How is Meg?" Olivia asked.

Dylan shrugged. "Exhausted. Scared. But she's resting, which is good."

Scott stepped forward. "Olivia filled me in. Did your friend file a police report about her assault?" the cop asked.

Dylan shook his head. "She doesn't think one shove is an assault." He ran a hand through his hair, frustrated by that.

Sympathy crossed the other man's face. "Do you want me to talk to her? At the very least, she can file for a restraining order. Maybe I can explain that to her."

Dylan gave the suggestion some thought. "I want to say no because it might upset her, but I'd rather she do something now than have the bastard try to come near her again."

Scott gestured with one hand. "Why don't you introduce me, and we'll go from there?"

Dylan glanced at Olivia. "Come with us," he said, unwilling to leave her alone or let her walk out on him again.

"Okay."

He led them to Meg's room and pushed the curtain aside. Meg's eyes opened at the sound. "Hey. I have someone I want you to talk to. Do you think you're up to it?" he asked.

Meg narrowed her gaze. "Who is it?"

"Olivia's brother Scott is a police officer," he said, bracing himself for her anger.

"Dylan!"

"Just let him explain your options. That's all I ask. What you do after that is up to you."

She leaned her head back on the stretcher the hospital called a bed. "Fine."

He turned and gestured for the other man to join him.

Scott pushed past the curtain and looked at Meg. If Dylan hadn't been watching the other man at the time, he'd have missed the complete look of interest on his face.

Meg, too, looked interested and perked up upon seeing the good-looking man.

"We're going to leave you two to talk," Dylan said. "Meg, you get some sleep. I'll come back in the morning to check on you. Let me know when they decide to discharge you. I'll pick you up and get you home."

He grasped Olivia's hand and tugged, leading her out of the room so they could have some time alone.

To Dylan's surprise, Olivia didn't argue when he told her he was driving them back to his place. She seemed more relaxed than he'd expected, and he figured he'd wait until they were in his apartment before bringing up the similarities between her past and Meg's present. And have yet another conversation that would, in all probability, go nowhere.

"Did you notice that Meg took one look at my brother and she was a goner?" she asked as he drove.

"I noticed the same thing about Scott. If that's the case, the man's going to have his hands full."

Olivia laughed. "Who knows? Meg is pregnant by a problem ex. She's probably not looking for anything with any man."

"Not to mention, Meg is drawn to bad boys. Not sure Scott fits the bill."

Olivia curled into her seat. "Meg needs a decent guy, and that's Scott. Assuming he's even into her."

"Why are we talking about a relationship between two people who don't even know each other?" Dylan muttered. Besides the obvious reason, that it was easier than discussing the unexpected turn their night had taken and the memories it must have dredged up for Olivia.

He pulled into the parking lot by his building and came around to her side of the car. "Want to walk on the beach?"

She glanced at him, surprised. "Sure."

They headed across the lot and around the back of the building, strolling down the long sidewalk before reaching the private entrance to the beach. Warm, humid air blew around them, something Dylan was more than used to from living in Florida for his entire life.

Olivia seemed entirely too calm and peaceful, which, in turn, amped up his nerves.

"Want to leave our shoes here?" she asked just as they were about to step on the sand.

"Works for me."

She pulled off the sandals she'd worn to the concert and rolled up her jeans to midcalf, and he followed her lead. They walked down the empty beach, the sand soft on his feet. He wanted to be relaxed, but he wasn't. First there was Meg, a woman he considered family, lying in a hospital bed, hoping to hold on to a baby she wanted, with an ex-boyfriend out there somewhere who'd hurt her.

Just like the night with Wendell, Meg's situation had reinforced for Dylan what was important in life. Family and having someone you could count on beside you. Those were the things that mattered. Meanwhile, Dylan walked alongside Olivia, a woman he wanted for his future . . . but she wasn't willing. And though he'd been telling himself he could hold out until she came around, he was growing more frustrated and tired by the day.

Olivia slipped her hand inside his, and instead of the contentment he usually found, his annoyance and anger grew. What more did he have to do to show her how he felt? What else did she need him to give her?

"Are you okay?" she asked at last.

"Fine. Why?"

"You're so stiff and quiet. It's just not like you."

He pulled to a halt.

Beside him, the water churned, and he stared out at the ocean. "I'm tired," he told her, no longer willing to couch his feelings in deference to hers. "I didn't realize it before tonight but . . . I'm tired of feeling like I'm the only one fighting for us."

She turned to face him, her skin pale in the moonlight, her expression grave. "If I were you, I'd be tired of me too." She slid her hands into her front pants pockets and rocked back and forth on her feet. "I never said I was easy, and you put up with my issues way longer than I had a right to expect you to."

She touched his cheek, and when he didn't react, she let her hand drop away.

He clenched his jaw, knowing whatever emotions were grinding away inside him needed to be let out. Let the chips fall where they might; he'd deal with the fallout later. "I don't want to give up on us, but—"

She held his gaze, not breaking eye contact. "I went to see a therapist," she said, blindsiding him.

"You did? When?"

"Remember the night I told you I was going to the movies? I went to an appointment with a doctor Madison recommended."

He didn't know whether to be happy or hurt. "Why didn't you tell me?" he asked, well aware hurt had won out.

She swallowed hard, her slender neck moving up and down. "I wasn't sure if I'd chicken out at the door," she admitted. "I tried to talk to someone after I lost the baby. It was too painful, and I didn't go back. I didn't want to disappoint you."

He ran a hand through his hair in frustration. "Hell, Liv, just knowing you were willing to make the effort would have gone a long way toward easing my mind."

"I should have been honest, but I also didn't say anything because I thought I might need time afterward. I didn't want to hurt you by saying I wanted to just go home alone."

"I'd like to think I would have understood. I also would have liked to know you were trying to work through things." He gritted his teeth, causing his jaw to ache. "So all this time I've been trying to hold us together, you were attempting to go it alone."

She blinked, those indigo eyes wide. "What? No! The whole reason I went to the doctor was because I wanted to make things work between *us*! I went for us. But when I left the office, I realized I needed to get help for myself most of all. *I* have to be able to move on from what happened."

He couldn't argue the point, but that didn't mean he liked how she'd handled things. "Sounds like you're starting to cope."

Without his help and without at least including him in her plans.

"It was only one appointment. I have a lot more to go, more work to do, but at least I told the doctor everything. I made a start."

She sounded proud of herself, and he ought to feel the same way. Hell, he probably would if his heart wasn't lodged somewhere in his throat.

What was she thinking? It was one of the first times between them that he really didn't have a clue. It had never dawned on him that when she was finally ready to move on, she might want to do it without him. He hadn't had that sense at the concert, but things with Meg had shifted his thinking. Maybe tonight had altered Olivia's perceptions too.

Was that what she was thinking of doing now? His chest ached at the notion.

"Tonight, when Meg said nearly losing this baby made her realize that she wanted to be a mother, that even if something happened with this pregnancy, she knew what she wanted . . . a lightbulb went on for me. Everything you tried to tell me became clear." Her eyes lit up with hope.

He didn't know if he could continue to listen to her explain her feelings while trying to form his own conclusions, none of them good. "Dammit, Olivia, what are you trying to say?"

"That you were right. I was looking at everything from the lens of my nineteen-year-old self. And she was a hurt, scared young girl. When I saw Meg, so brave and unafraid to cope with whatever came . . . it hit me. I still want all those same things I used to dream about." She grasped his hand, holding him tight against her chest. "I want a house, white picket fence, dog, kids, all of it. With you," she said, repeating his words back to him.

She looked up at him with all the love and hope he'd ever wanted to see reflected in her eyes and in her expression, and relief rushed at him as fast as the ocean waves. "Jesus, Liv."

She shrugged. "What can I say? I know I'm not easy. Okay, I admit I'm pretty high maintenance." Her luscious lips curved upward in a smile. "But I hope you still think I'm worth it."

"You're not only worth it, sunshine. You're everything. You always were and you always will be."

He swung her into his arms, and she locked her legs around his waist, settling her exactly where she belonged. His heart lifted at the change in her, at the possibilities the future offered. He didn't kid himself that the tough times were over or that she had gotten past all her issues just like that. But she was open and willing and getting help. That was all he'd ever wanted.

"One thing I know for sure—life with you will never be boring."

"Well, I should hope not."

He nuzzled his cheek against hers. "Whatever happens from now on, we handle it together, do you understand?"

She nodded, hugging him back with a desperation he appreciated, given that he'd been convinced he was about to lose her for good.

"And if you're pregnant, we're in this the same way. Together. Right?" he asked.

Once more, she nodded, but she didn't peel them apart to look at him or speak.

"What do you say we go home?"

"Home?" she squeaked, this time easing back so she could see his face.

"Home. That big apartment upstairs, for now. Until I can get started on the house, the white picket fence, and the dog." Because he wasn't letting her out of his sight for a good long while. Okay, not ever.

"Is that your inelegant way of asking me to move in with you?" She raised one eyebrow.

"No way, baby. I'm not asking. I'm insisting. When I buy the ring, which will be first chance I get, then I'll *ask* you to marry me."

"Maybe you should just insist on that too. You know I like it when you're bossy."

She shifted her hips, her sex brushing against his awakening erection, and he groaned.

He thought about it and shrugged. Why wait? "Olivia Dare, you're not only moving in, you're marrying me. Any objections?"

"Not one." She grinned, clearly happy and as invested in their future as he was.

Finally.

Epilogue

"Tell me why I said I wanted to do this again?" Olivia asked, moaning as she climbed back into bed from another trip to the bathroom. Another round of morning sickness. Another time she'd brushed her teeth and promised herself it would be the last time for a good long while.

Dylan pushed her hair off her face and kissed her forehead. "Are you sure you don't want to call Ian and Riley and tell them we can't make it?"

She shook her head. "You've never met my New York cousins, and I really want you to get to know them."

"Only if you're up to it."

She managed a smile. "I am. I feel better already."

"Liar."

"Is that any way to talk to the soon-to-be mother of your child?" Sure enough, the second time in her life she'd been stupid about protection, she'd ended up pregnant.

"You're also my wife."

She grinned, holding up her left hand with the diamond ring and the matching wedding band beneath. "I sure am."

Once given the green light, Dylan had moved fast. Within a week of her turnaround, they'd been engaged. And no sooner had she discovered she was pregnant than they'd eloped to Las Vegas, taking a page from Madison and Alex's playbook. Unlike Alex, she'd invited her mother and any siblings

176

available at the last minute, so there were no upset relatives to deal with afterward.

He rolled onto his side and gazed at her. "I love you."

"I know." He'd proved it over and over, sticking by her when a lesser man would have given up. "I love you too."

"Do you have any idea how sexy you are?" he asked.

"Oh yes, I do. Nauseous and pale, I'm lovely." Blech. At least she was nearing the end of her first trimester. The end of the nausea was in sight. She hoped.

A scowl formed on his handsome face. "Your breasts are bigger, your face is as gorgeous as ever, and my baby is growing in here." He slid his hand over her belly, a habit he'd discovered pretty quickly. "Sexy," he confirmed.

"I'm glad you think so. It's pretty unfair how easily men get off during this whole thing."

"Baby, I went to the nearest minimart at eleven p.m. last night looking for mint chocolate chip ice cream. It's not that easy."

"But I thanked you in the best possible way, didn't I?" she asked, her voice thick with the memory of eating that ice cream off his erection. Thank goodness her morning sickness stuck to the morning hours.

He let out a low growl at the reminder, reaching for her, but she scooted backward fast. "I have to shower if we're going to get to Ian's on time."

He laid his arm over his eyes. "Go," he said with a groan.

She laughed and headed for the shower, feeling better already.

A little while later, they walked into Ian's house, where her entire family had already gathered. "Are you okay?" she asked Dylan, knowing he wasn't used to the huge family chaos all the Dares tended to bring.

"More than okay." He squeezed her hand.

Without warning, a loud screech sounded, followed by a toddler barreling toward Olivia. "Auntie Liv!"

Olivia held out her arms, and the little girl tripped, falling into her. Olivia scooped up her niece and planted a smacking kiss on her cheek. "How's my favorite girl?" she asked.

Rainey Noelle, Ian and Riley's daughter, clasped Olivia's cheeks in her chubby hands and gave her a smacking kiss right back. That was their routine, one they'd developed when Olivia had started visiting her niece weekly. It hadn't been easy at first, getting past her fear of losing what meant the most to her. With the help of her therapist and Dylan, Olivia was becoming more secure, both with herself and the people she loved.

Dylan's hand on her back steadied her now, as he always did.

"There you are!" Riley strode out of the kitchen, heading toward them. "Hi, Dylan, Liv." She kissed them each. "You were in the middle of eating," she reminded the little girl. "Come back to Mommy. You can play with Auntie Liv later." Riley held out her hands, and Rainey fell into her mother's arms.

The child was fearless in everything she did and drove Ian to distraction. Olivia loved seeing her formerly stoic big brother wrapped around a child's little fingers.

"Everyone's in the kitchen except the boys. Tyler, Scott, and Jason are shooting baskets out back," Riley said, turning and carrying her daughter back the way she'd come.

Olivia led Dylan into the fray. He already knew all the Miami siblings. Ian and Riley stood together in one corner, struggling to get Rainey into her high chair.

Her father was nowhere to be found. Olivia would like to think it was out of respect for her mother, Emma, that he and Savannah stayed away. But the truth was, Robert Dare would always do what was best for him. The other truth was that Emma had moved on long ago. She was here with her *special friend*, as she called Michael Brooks, the man she'd been seeing for a while now. He stood along with their mom, talking to Avery.

"I don't like how sad Avery looks," Olivia whispered to Dylan. "Something's been off since that concert a few months ago, and she won't talk to me about it."

"You, of all people, know what it's like to need to work things out on your own," he reminded her.

She scowled at him, disliking the reminder. "Fine. But I'm keeping an eye on her."

He shook his head and grinned. "I'd expect nothing less."

"Have you met Sienna?" she asked of her half sister, who waved from across the room.

"At your birthday party."

She waved back and held up one finger, indicating she'd come see her in a minute. She grasped Dylan's hand and led him to the great room off the kitchen.

"Olivia!" Gabe's wife, Isabelle, called her name. Next thing Olivia knew, she was engulfed in an exuberant Izzy hug. "How are you? And congratulations on your wedding! Is this Dylan?"

Olivia grinned. "Yes, Dylan, this is Isabelle. And that man over there with the baby in his arms is my cousin Gabe." He raised a hand in greeting from his seat on the couch.

"The similar-looking guy next to him is his brother, Decklan," Olivia said, raising her voice so her cousin would pay attention. "Decklan's a cop in New York. He and Scott usually hang out and compare notes."

Sure enough, at the loud mention of his name, Decklan turned his head. "Hey, Liv." He rose to his feet just as his girlfriend, Amanda, walked over, two drinks in hand. "Here you go." She handed him one, and together, they joined Isabelle.

Introductions and hugs followed.

"Lucy, their sister, couldn't make it. She was tied up on a nightclub job."

"I hope to meet her another time," Dylan said.

"Me too. You'll love her."

Meanwhile, Dylan shook Decklan's hand, then said hello to the women before glancing at Gabe. "I'd love to talk to you about your nightclubs," Dylan said.

He kissed Olivia on the lips, and she barely managed a soft moan at the sexy feel of his goatee against her skin.

"Go ahead," she told him, happy he was comfortable with her large family. She wished his sister had been able to join them, but she and Matthew had had other plans.

He and Decklan settled in with Gabe, while Olivia stood with the women.

"Amanda, how do you like living in New York?" Olivia asked, knowing she had moved from the Maryland/Washington, DC, area to live with Decklan.

"It's great. I'm really happy and . . ." She held out her hand. "Decklan and I are engaged!"

"Congratulations!" Olivia said, pulling her into a hug. "I'm so happy for you! So when's the big day?"

"We're still trying to work out the where and when," Amanda said.

"But soon," Decklan called out. "Because I'm not waiting much longer."

Amanda blushed.

Before Olivia could respond, her brothers stomped in from the garage, all fighting for who could get to the bar with the soda and drinks first. They elbowed and joked with each other, but Scott seemed more subdued.

"Excuse me a minute," she said to her cousins' wives.

She walked over to Scott, pulling him aside. "Hey."

"Hey, sis. What's going on with you?" he asked.

She shrugged. "Just enjoying family time. How about you?"

"Kicking brotherly ass on the court."

She rolled her eyes at the typical comment.

"I need to ask you something," Scott said.

"Name it."

"How's Meg?"

Olivia blew out a long breath, not surprised her brother had brought up her name. "You didn't keep in touch?"

He shook his head. "I helped her through the restraining order after she was released from the hospital."

Meg had been put on temporary bed rest, but once things with her pregnancy had stabilized, she'd gone back to work.

"But any time I reached out afterward, she said she was fine and shut me down."

"You actually asked her out?" Olivia asked.

Scott nodded. "She *says* she's not interested." He frowned at that, his expression indicating he wasn't convinced Meg was telling the truth.

Olivia wasn't buying it either. Meg had asked her about Scott too. But whenever the topic of men or dating came up, Meg said that she'd always been too dependent on the opposite sex to take care of her. She was tired of being needy and of picking the wrong men just to have someone in her life. She was also finished relying on men who were her friends. She'd been talking about Dylan.

Olivia understood that Meg wanted to change, to become more independent and self-reliant. She just didn't think that meant closing herself off to romance altogether.

She glanced at her brother. "Before I give you any advice, I have a question."

Scott leaned against the counter. "I'm listening."

"You do realize Meg is pregnant, right?"

Her brother burst out laughing. "You didn't just ask me that."

She rolled her eyes. "That's not how I meant it, you doofus! I meant, she's going to have a *baby*. You can't go after Meg just because you think she's hot. A woman like Meg means serious commitment and—"

His dark scowl told Olivia all she needed to know. "Fine! You get the situation." And he was still interested. "Then my advice is not to give up." She bit the inside of her cheek. "Look at me and Dylan. We wouldn't be together today if he'd listened to what I *said* I wanted." And thank God for that. "Dylan looked deeper, got to know me first, and understood I was hiding from myself. He was determined to win."

"Huh." Scott paused in thought. "So insert myself in her life whether she wants it or not?"

Olivia smacked her brother on the side of the head.

"Ouch!"

"Then don't be an idiot and pay attention! Be there for Meg. Make yourself useful, and see what's behind those walls she puts up. If the feelings are mutual, then you'll know what to do."

Scott grinned, then wrapped his arms around Olivia, picking her up off her feet.

"Put me down!" she squealed.

He did as she asked. "Thank you."

She nodded. "Meg would be lucky to get a guy like you. But I love you, and I don't want to see you get hurt either."

Scott shrugged off her concern. "I already know Meg likes me. I can handle the rest," he said, ever her cocky sibling, as he strode off.

Olivia headed back to Dylan and the New York contingent and seated herself between Dylan and Gabe.

"Hey." Dylan wrapped an arm around her, and she leaned into him, savoring his embrace.

"Gabe, are you going to share the little prince?" she asked of the baby boy he hadn't yet pawned off on his mother.

"Gabriel, give the baby to your cousin," Isabelle said from behind him.

Olivia did her best not to laugh, but she did hold out her arms.

Gabe reluctantly parted with his son, handing her the little boy.

She held the baby close to her chest. "Hey, Noah," she said to the sleeping baby, taking in his tiny, already handsome features. "You're going to be a heartbreaker like the rest of the Dare men."

She bent her head, inhaling his baby smell. For the first time, no pangs of what might have been hit her. Instead, she was surrounded by what was—her big, loving, ever-expanding family. A new husband she adored and who would do everything in his power to always be there for her, and a baby of her own on the way.

Which reminded her. Somehow she'd managed to keep her pregnancy a secret from everyone except her mother and Avery. She wanted the first few months to pass, to know that this time would be different. From the awful morning sickness, it already was, she thought wryly.

But now, with her whole family gathered, she was ready.

Ever perceptive, Dylan leaned in and whispered in her ear. "All good?" he asked.

"All great," she said back. "And I guess this is as good a time as any to let them know."

Dylan squeezed her tight.

"I have an announcement," she said loudly.

It took a while, but her family finally quieted down.

"I'm pregnant," she told them all.

The ensuing chaos, clapping, and congratulations told her what she already knew. What Olivia Rhodes had in her life was good. Really, really good. She wanted that good to continue, not just for herself, but for everyone she loved. Every sibling and cousin in this room.

The Dare to Love Series continues with
Dare to Hold, Book #4

Dare to Love Series

Turn the page to start reading *Dare to Hold* excerpt!

Chapter One

Some women always managed to get it right. To make the right choices, to pick the right man, to nail this crazy thing called life. Meg Thompson, on the other hand, managed to end up single and pregnant. But she couldn't regret the baby growing inside her, and from now on, she was determined to get things right.

She pulled on her favorite pair of jeans, tugged them up over her hips, and unsuccessfully attempted to close the button. She grunted and laid down on the bed, pulling the sides closer together, but no luck. She wriggled, sucked in a deep breath, and tried again, only to end up huffing out a stream of air in frustration.

"Didn't these fit just last weekend?" she asked herself, peeling the denim off her legs and tossing them onto the floor with a groan.

She glanced down at her still-flat stomach, placing her hand over her belly. "How can something I can't see or feel cause so much upheaval in my life?" And how could she love the baby growing inside her so much already?

A vibrating buzz told her someone was sending her a message. She checked her phone.

Lizzy: Almost ready?

Meg sighed. Her best friend, Elizabeth Cooper, was due to pick her up in ten minutes. Girls' night out. Or, in Lizzy's words, hookup night and Meg's last chance for a hot, no-holds-barred fling before she started to show and her sole focus became being a new mom. Meg was up for girls' night, but no way would she be picking up a stranger for a one-night stand. Her days of choosing the wrong men were over. Mike was the last in a long line of sucky choices. So not only did she not trust her judgment when it came to the opposite sex, but it no longer mattered. She was finished relying on men to define her or make her happy.

"Right, baby?" She patted her belly and headed to her closet for a pair of elastic-waist leggings.

Meg and her friends settled into their seats at Mel's, a popular spot for casual drinks after work and on the weekends. Mel's was a dimly lit bistro with a wood-fired oven and grill in the back, dark mahogany-looking tables throughout, and a funky bar where people gathered. Meg loved it here.

She waved to the waiter, who stepped over to their table.

"What can I get you ladies?"

The girls ordered alcoholic drinks, and the good-looking waiter turned to Meg.

"I'll have a club soda. With a lime."

"Going for the hard stuff, I see." He winked and scribbled down her order.

Meg smiled. "Designated driver." Which wasn't a lie. Lizzy might have picked her up, but Meg would be the one driving home.

She glanced around at the women she'd ignored for a long time in favor of her asshole ex and, unfortunately, her baby daddy. She was grateful these women were here for her now, because Meg had a bad habit of dropping friends in favor of men. Men she looked to for the love and acceptance she'd never received from a father she barely remembered. Meg sighed and rested her chin on her hands. Her childhood memories included a string of her mother's boyfriends who came and went from her young life.

Her mother had set a pattern Meg unconsciously followed. First she'd latched on to Dylan Rhodes, the one and only good guy in her life. He'd been her high school boyfriend and her rock until they broke up before going to college, and then Meg began emulating her mother's taste by choosing men who always took advantage one way or another.

Luckily, she and Dylan had reconnected when they'd moved back to Miami years later, but Meg had overrelied on Dylan instead of standing on her own two feet. It took Dylan falling hard for another woman to wake Meg up to her too-needy ways. Dylan was her friend, but he was now Olivia Dare's husband. And Meg was determined to be independent. Everything the way it should be.

"Earth to Meg." Lizzy waved a hand in front of her eyes.

Meg blinked, startled. "Sorry. Just got lost there for a minute."

"Nowhere good, from the look on your face." Lizzy tilted her head to one side, her long blonde curls falling over her shoulder. "Everything okay?" Her friend studied her, her brown eyes soft and concerned.

Meg smiled. "Couldn't be better. I was actually thinking about the changes I've made—that I'm determined to keep making in my life. And it's really good to be out with you guys," Meg said, meaning it.

"It's great to be out with you too," Lizzy said.

The waiter stopped by the table and passed out their beverages. Meg took a long sip of her cold soda, appreciating the way it eased her dry throat.

"Well, you must be doing something right because you're glowing," Lizzy said.

"It's the pregnancy hormones," Meg muttered.

"No, seriously. You look beautiful," her friend insisted.

Meg smiled at her. "Thank you."

Allie Mendez, the office secretary at Meg's school, and the third woman in their posse, slipped her cell into her purse and leaned closer to join the conversation. "Maybe I should get myself pregnant, because Lizzy's right. You're gorgeous."

Meg blushed. "And you two need glasses."

"Not if the guys at the next table are any indication. Look. The blond one can't take his eyes off you!" Lizzy said, her voice rising in excitement.

Oh no. All Lizzy needed was a target and she'd be aiming Meg his way all night. "I'm sure he's looking at one of you. Not the pregnant woman in the elastic-waist pants." Lizzy with her blonde beauty or Allie and her olive skin and luscious curves attracted men wherever they went.

"You must not have looked in a mirror before leaving the house," Allie told her, a frown on her pretty face.

"Oh, look! He's coming this way. Now remember. There's nothing wrong with getting yourself some before your life gets serious." Lizzy nudged her arm.

"I don't want some," Meg muttered. "If he's so hot, you should—"

"Hi, ladies," the man said, bracing an arm on the back of Meg's chair.

"Hi!" Lizzy said too brightly.

"My friends and I would like to buy you all a drink." He spoke to the table, but his eyes were on Meg.

She shook her head. "We were just having a private convers—"

"We'd like that," Allie chimed in.

"Mind if we join you then?" he asked, making Meg wonder if he was dense, oblivious, or just that ego-driven.

In response, Lizzy slid her chair away from Meg, making room for the other man to sit. Which, after grabbing his chair and pulling it over to the table, he did. His pals joined them too.

Meg shot her friend an annoyed look.

"Give him a chance," Lizzy mouthed behind the man's back.

Rob, Mark, and Ken, they said their names as conversation began to flow. Ken was the one closest to Meg, and with his light hair and coloring, he definitely resembled his Barbie-doll namesake. Even if she were interested in a hookup, a preppy man who liked to talk about himself wouldn't be her choice. She disliked his wandering hands even more.

He brushed her back.

She stiffened.

He sat forward so their shoulders touched. She shoved her chair in the opposite direction.

Somehow he ended up close beside her again, his thigh touching hers.

She was all too ready to go home, but her friends seemed to like the guys they were talking to, and she didn't want to ruin their time by being rude to Ken. She wouldn't leave with him, but she'd be pleasant while they were here.

"So what do you do for a living?" he asked.

"I'm a kindergarten teacher."

He blinked, long lashes framing green eyes. "That's . . . brave."

"Don't like kids?" she asked none too sweetly.

He fake-shuddered. "Not for a good long while. But you must have a decent pension plan?" he asked, back on the subject he liked best. Ken was a stockbroker and investor, and soon she found herself listening to all the ways she could save more money by investing with the best of the best. Him, of course.

She hid a yawn behind her hand, and when her bladder informed her she needed a trip to the restroom, she nearly groaned out loud in relief.

"If you'll excuse me, I need to go . . . freshen up. I'll be back in a few minutes." Meg rose, and Ken followed, helping her pull out her chair.

Allie met her gaze. "Gentleman," she mouthed in approval.

Meg swallowed a groan.

"I'll be waiting," Ken said as she walked away.

"Oh, please don't be," she said to herself, making her way to the bathroom at the far back of the restaurant.

She spent a long time in the restroom, checking her phone, swiping some gloss on her dry lips, and washing her hands, twice, in her effort to stall returning to the table.

When she did, she paused by Lizzy's chair and whispered in her friend's ear, "I'm going to bail. I'm not up to this. I'm really sorry. Will you be okay driving?"

"Of course. I barely had a sip. But I can leave and take you home."

She shook her head. "No need. You seem to be hitting it off with Mark. I can get Uber," she said.

"I'd be happy to drive you," Ken said.

She hadn't realized he'd left his seat and had overheard them.

"No, really. Stay and have fun. I'm just not feeling too well." Which was a lie, but it was nicer than *Go away, I'm not interested.*

Which was ironic since, not too long ago, Meg would have been all too willing to see where things went with a guy who showed her any interest at all. Maybe the baby really was changing her, making her more self-reliant and aware as well as giving her better taste in men.

"Then you really shouldn't go home alone," Ken said, grasping her forearm.

Oh no he didn't. She pinned him with an annoyed glare. "Let. Go." And what was it about her that attracted assholes anyway? she asked herself as she tried to extricate herself without resorting to insults or calling management.

Lizzy jumped up from her seat just as the jerk released her arm and a familiar voice reverberated in her ear.

"Touch her again and you'll answer to me."

Scott Dare arrived at Mel's and found his brother Tyler waiting for him at the bar. He and Tyler often hung out at Mel's on Scott's rare nights off duty. He was a cop, and after disobeying a direct order by going into a situation without backup, he was currently enjoying administrative leave. He was chafing under the rules and no longer finding the same satisfaction in the job as he once had. Meeting with his brother was the highlight of his week so far.

Scott tipped his beer back and took a long pull.

"So seriously, what's up your ass other than boredom?" Tyler asked.

"Boredom isn't enough?" Scott scanned the room, his gaze landing on a table of women he hadn't noticed before that included one very familiar face. His boredom instantly vanished.

Any time he saw Meg Thompson, every part of him took notice, and tonight was no exception. He didn't know what it was about her. Her brown hair was just that. Brown silk that hung just below her shoulders, but there were highlights that turned some parts a sexy reddish-blonde under the right light. Brown eyes the color of his morning coffee framed by thick lashes that too often showed a vulnerability she tried hard to hide. It was that forced strength that got to him. She was alone, dealing with a difficult situation that would break most women.

But she wasn't like any other woman he'd met. And completely unlike Scott's ex-wife.

"Do you know them?" Tyler tipped his head toward the table of women.

"I know the brunette." Scott rose . . . only to find a blond guy had beat him to it. The man leaned closer to Meg, and Scott stiffened, forcing himself to sit down and watch.

"Who is she?" his brother asked.

"She's Dylan's friend, Meg Thompson."

"Aah. Liv told me about her. She thought Meg would be a problem when she got involved with Dylan, but they ended up being friends."

Scott nodded. "That's her."

"And I'm guessing you two have history since you can't take your eyes off of her?" Tyler nudged him in the side.

"Yes. No. Shit," he muttered, wondering how to explain his reaction to Meg.

From the minute Scott had seen her, looking small and defenseless in a hospital bed after nearly losing her baby thanks to her angry ex-boyfriend, Scott had been invested. Not even her pregnancy had put him off. Which, all things considered, should scare the shit out of him. Since Leah, he didn't get seriously involved.

He'd questioned Meg, taken her statement, and guided her through the restraining order process. And he'd been dumb enough to try to help. To be there for her afterward, but she wasn't interested. Not in a helping hand.

Not in him.

He'd been forced to see her at occasional get-togethers at Olivia and Dylan's over the last month, had run into her in the supermarket. He'd offered to take her to dinner, to be her friend. Despite the undeniable chemistry between them, she'd declined.

Two other men joined the first, and soon the women at Meg's table were paired off. And Scott was pissed. A low growl escaped his throat.

"Easy, bro." Instead of giving him a hard time, Tyler placed a hand on his shoulder.

Scott blew out a long breath. Logically, he knew he didn't have a say in what Meg did. Or with whom.

He ordered a Patrón. Neat. And settled in to do what he did best. Keep an eye on her from a distance. To his relief, as time passed, she didn't look at all interested in the guy. Her body language screamed *don't touch*, and the asshole didn't appear to be listening.

"I'm going to bash his head in if this keeps up," Scott muttered.

Tyler raised an eyebrow. "First Ian, now you. Are you really going to leave me as the only single Dare guy in the family?"

"She's made it clear she's not interested in me, and besides, marriage? Been there, have the divorce papers to show for it. Not happening again," Scott reminded his brother. At twenty-nine, he was finished with that stupid dream. Leah had screwed with his head on so many levels he was lucky he wasn't still dizzy two years later.

He had no intention of letting his brother in on the fact that Meg was pregnant. His sibling would have a field day with Scott's interest based on that alone. He'd be wrong. But it wasn't worth the hassle or discussion.

"Sorry," Tyler muttered, obviously uncomfortable.

Scott wasn't sure if he was referring to the divorce, the reason behind it, or Meg's lack of interest. All were enough to shit on his ego.

Meg shoved her chair back and headed for the back of the restaurant, where the restrooms were located, and Scott breathed easily for the first time since realizing she was there.

"You going after her?" Tyler asked.

"No."

"It's not like you to give up when you want something."

Good point, Scott thought, but he remained seated. Watching but wary.

Meg returned and stopped by one of her friends, whispering something in her ear. The women spoke, and suddenly the guy who'd been inching closer to her all evening walked up to them. They talked. Looked more like an argument.

And then he grabbed Meg's arm. Scott bolted out of his seat and came up behind Meg. Her soft scent invaded his senses, but his focus was on the asshole who hadn't released her.

"Let. Go," Meg said through clenched teeth.

Scott's hands fisted at his sides. "Touch her again and you'll answer to me."

Meg didn't know where Scott Dare had come from. She hadn't noticed him in the bar earlier, and she was always aware when he was near. How could she not be? He was everything that appealed to her in a man. Tall, with jet-black hair that always looked as if he'd just run his hand through the inky strands. Full lips. Straight nose. So damned handsome.

Though he had a dominant streak a mile wide, one she couldn't miss during their few encounters, he'd been warm and caring when taking her statement in the hospital. And he was a cop, which meant he wasn't her typical bad boy, but he gave off a masculine vibe that just did it for her.

"Who the hell are you?" Ken asked Scott, interrupting her blatant perusal.

"A friend who heard her tell you to get lost." If Scott's pissed-off tone and much bigger build wasn't enough to make his point, he pushed his jacket back, revealing his holstered gun. "I'm off duty, but it still works."

Ken raised both hands and took a step back. "Easy, man. It's not my fault she gave off the wrong signals." He shook his head and stormed off, his friends pushing their chairs back and quickly following.

"Are you okay?" Lizzy asked, her hand protectively on Meg's arm.

"I'm fine."

"And who is this?" Allie asked, coming up on Meg's other side.

She tipped her head toward Scott, still not meeting his gaze. She wasn't ready. "Liz, Allie, this is Scott Dare."

"Holy hell, girl," Allie whispered none too softly. "I can see why you weren't interested in the Ken doll."

Meg's cheeks burned.

"Nice to meet you both," Scott said in that voice that Meg heard in her dreams.

He turned toward her, giving her no choice but to look into those sexy navy—almost violet—eyes, made more vibrant by his light-blue shirt. "Meg, a word?"

She shook her head. She'd managed to put him out of her thoughts, which hadn't been easy, and here he was, coming to her rescue and making demands. If she wasn't so determined to turn over a new leaf, be independent, she'd respond to his sexy tone and probably do anything he asked. Her damp panties were proof of that.

"I was just telling my friends I'm going home." She kissed Lizzy on the cheek and squeezed Allie's hand, reassuring them both she was fine.

She strode past Scott, knowing full well he'd follow. He waited until they were on the street away from the crowds before he grasped her hand and turned her to face him. "Meg."

"Thank you for getting rid of the creep." She pulled her phone from her bag and scrolled for the app that would let her call for a car.

"I'll drive you home."

"Was that an offer or an order?" she asked, unable to help her sarcastic mouth. He brought that out in her.

He shot her a look. One that had her quivering inside. And giving in to his demand. "Okay, you can drive me home."

And then she planned to walk herself inside, close her front door, and forget about Scott Dare.

Without a word, he grasped her elbow and led her to a parking lot where his Range Rover was parked.

"I can't believe what a mess tonight turned out to be," she muttered once they were settled in the plush leather seats.

"What were you doing there in the first place?"

She swung around to face him. "I can't go out to a restaurant with friends?"

"Of course you can."

He wanted to say more. She could tell from the tense set of his jaw.

She sighed and decided to save him the trouble. "No, you're right. Lizzy and Allie had this idea of taking me out so

I could pick up a guy and have one last fling before I start to show." She slid her hands over her stomach. "And before I'm busy being a mom."

His grip on the steering wheel tightened. "You were going to hook up with some stranger?" he asked through gritted teeth.

"What? No! I said they thought I should. I just went out to see my friends. Then that guy sat down and—Why am I explaining myself to you?" she asked, trailing off.

But it had been this way with Scott from the first time they'd met. She found him easy to talk to. Understanding. Like he heard what she said and cared, unlike her ex. Or any of the men in her past.

She watched the palm trees and scenery as he drove. She'd already told him where she lived when she'd explained how she'd ended up in the hospital a little over a month ago. She just couldn't believe he remembered. All too soon, they reached their destination. He pulled into a parking spot at her apartment complex.

He put the truck in park, cut the engine, and turned to face her. "You talk to me because you know that you can trust me."

Point proven. He remembered what she'd said at least five minutes ago.

"But I hardly know you."

"Instinct."

She shook her head at that. "Mine's failed me many times before." And miserably, at that, she thought.

"Not this time." He let himself out of the truck and started to walk around to her side.

Realizing his intent, she opened the door and hopped out just as he reached her. He shut the door behind her. "Let's go."

"I can see myself up."

"You could. But since I took you home, I'll get you safely to your door."

He slid a hand to the small of her back, and she felt his heated palm through the fabric of her top. Goose bumps prickled along her skin.

She lived in a first-floor apartment, and they reached her door. He turned her around to face him. "Your friends want you to have one last fling? Is that what you want too?"

She hadn't given a fling any thought. Not until Scott said the word, a husky bent to his voice and determined intent behind his words. "I don't want sex with some random stranger."

She glanced up and found herself pinned by his stare. His lips lifted in a sexy grin. "I'm not a stranger."

She opened then closed her mouth as she processed his words and the meaning behind them. He wasn't a stranger. Not really. He knew more about her than most people, and her best friends could vouch for him.

She ran her tongue over her dry lips. His darkening gaze deliberately followed the movement, and her body responded, nipples puckering beneath the cotton of her shirt. He wanted a fling. Sex. With her.

And she wanted him, every rock-hard inch of his toned, muscled body. Had from the very first moment she'd seen him and every time since. She'd evaded him, certain that was the right thing to do for herself and for her baby, because she had new standards and rules she had to follow for her own sanity and for her future. But this *thing* between them wasn't going away. If anything, it was becoming more intense, growing more heated, and she couldn't deny it or walk away from him again.

"I'm not interested in a relationship," she reminded him.

He inclined his head. "And I'm not asking for one. Not even asking for a date this time."

"Just a fling?" she repeated, thinking he had to be kidding. Just like she'd thought he was kidding when he'd asked her out before. Because what would a hot, good-looking man like Scott Dare want with a woman who'd gotten herself knocked up and then pushed around by her ex-boyfriend?

Even when she'd realized Scott was serious about dating, she couldn't accept. Because she could so easily see herself repeating old patterns with him. Falling hard and fast. Giving in. Losing herself. And now there was more at stake than just Meg.

But this time, Scott was offering something she could handle. A night with a beginning and an end, no expectations. No disturbing her resolution to stand on her own. To be a better mother than her own had been, no revolving door of men. No man, period. Just a hot night and a memory to keep her warm when she was alone.

"One night." He reached out and rubbed his thumb across her lower lip.

His touch made her tremble, and her nipples tightened into hardened points, and the intensity in his gorgeous eyes had need building even stronger inside her.

"Is that what you want too?" he asked again, his gaze hot on hers.

His distinctive scent, a hint of musk she associated with Scott alone, filled her nostrils. Her stomach fluttered, and the desire to wrap herself around him and take what he offered built until it was a tangible thing, living and breathing inside her tightly strung body.

She nodded, unable to speak. Her throat had grown too dry.

"I need you to say it."

Say what? She didn't remember his question. Only the thought of letting him into her apartment . . . into her body filled her mind and her senses.

A low rumble sounded from deep inside his chest. "Say *I want you, Scott.* I need the words, or I'll send you inside alone."

"I want you, Scott." The words tumbled out, an easy capitulation that had been anything but. Another Meg Thompson decision she feared would alter the course of her life. And she was powerless to stop it.

Get *Dare to Hold* now at your
local bookstore or buy online!

ABOUT THE AUTHOR

Carly Phillips is the *New York Times* and *USA Today* bestselling author of more than fifty sexy contemporary romance novels featuring hot men, strong women, and the emotionally compelling stories her readers have come to expect and love. Carly's career spans over a decade and a half with various New York publishing houses, and she is now an indie author who runs her own business and loves every exciting minute of her publishing journey. Carly is  happily married to her college sweetheart and is the mother of two nearly adult daughters and three crazy dogs (two wheaten terriers and one mutant Havanese) who star on her Facebook fan page and website. Carly loves social media and is always around to interact with her readers. You can find out more about Carly at www.carlyphillips.com.

Carly's Booklist by Series

Dare to Love Series
Book 1: *Dare to Love* (Ian & Riley)
Book 2: *Dare to Desire*
(Alex & Madison)
Book 3: *Dare to Touch*
(Olivia & Dylan)
Book 4: *Dare to Hold* (Scott & Meg)
Book 5: *Dare to Rock* (Avery & Grey)
Book 6: *Dare to Take* (Tyler & Ella)

NY Dares Series
Book 1: *Dare to Surrender*
(Gabe & Isabelle)
Book 2: *Dare to Submit*
(Decklan & Amanda)
Book 3: *Dare to Seduce*
(Max & Lucy)

*The NY Dares books are
more erotic/hotter books.

Serendipity Series
Serendipity
Destiny
Karma

Serendipity's Finest Series
Perfect Fit
Perfect Fling
Perfect Together

Serendipity Novellas
Fated
Hot Summer Nights
(Perfect Stranger)

Bachelor Blog Series
Kiss Me If You Can
Love Me If You Dare

Lucky Series
Lucky Charm
Lucky Streak
Lucky Break

Ty and Hunter Series
Cross My Heart
Sealed with a Kiss

Hot Zone Series
Hot Stuff
Hot Number
Hot Item
Hot Property

Costas Sisters Series
Summer Lovin'
Under the Boardwalk

Chandler Brothers Series
The Bachelor
The Playboy
The Heartbreaker

Stand-Alone Titles
Brazen
Seduce Me
Secret Fantasy
The Right Choice
Suddenly Love
Perfect Partners
Unexpected Chances
Worthy of Love

Keep up with Carly and her upcoming books:

Website
www.carlyphillips.com

Sign up for blog and website updates
www.carlyphillips.com/category/blog/

Sign up for Carly's newsletter
www.carlyphillips.com/newsletter-sign-up

Carly on Facebook
www.facebook.com/CarlyPhillipsFanPage

Carly on Twitter
www.twitter.com/carlyphillips

Hang out at Carly's Corner—hot guys & giveaways!
smarturl.it/CarlysCornerFB

CPSIA information can be obtained
at www.ICGtesting.com
Printed in the USA
LVOW11s0824090317
526579LV00001B/1/P